BEING
STALKED

BEING
STALKED

A Memoir

ROBERT FINE

1945—

Chatto & Windus
London

Published in 1997

1 3 5 7 9 10 8 6 4 2

Copyright © 1997 by Robert Fine

Robert Fine has asserted his right under
the Copyright, Designs and Patents Act, 1988
to be identified as the author of this work.

First published in Great Britain in 1997 by
Chatto & Windus Limited
Random House, 20 Vauxhall Bridge Road,
London, SW1V 2SA

Random House Australia (Pty) Limited
20 Alfred Street, Milsons Point, Sydney,
New South Wales 2061, Australia

Random House New Zealand Limited
18 Poland Road, Glenfield
Auckland 10, New Zealand

Random House South Africa (Pty) Limited
P O Box 337, Bergvlei, South Africa

Random House UK Limited Reg. No. 954009

Papers used by Random House UK Limited are natural, recyclable
products made from wood grown in sustainable forests. The
manufacturing processes conform to the environmental
regulations of the country of origin.

A CIP catalogue record for this book
is available from the British Library

ISBN 0 7011 6685 1

Typeset by Deltatype, Birkenhead, Wirral
Printed and bound in Great Britain by
Mackays of Chatham PLC, Chatham, Kent

To Gillian Rose and Shoshi

We don't see the human eye as a receiver; it seems not [to] let something in, but to send it out. The ear receives; the eye looks. (It casts glances, it flashes, beams, coruscates.) With the eye one may terrify, not with the ear or the nose. When you see the eye, you see something go out from it. You see the glance of the eye.

Wittgenstein, *Remarks on the Philosophy of Psychology*

We must distinguish between two things: what is established by law and what I have discovered through personel experience; you must not confuse the two.

Kafka, *The Trial*

Contents

Preface

Diary Extract: Thursday 16 November 1995
My fiftieth birthday! Mrs M waited for me outside the swimming pool at about 8 a.m. and then followed me into the pool. I then saw her walking outside my house, on the pavement, about 9.30 a.m.

Stalking is a crime of the 1990s. Its roots lie in America. In the 1980s it had barely been visible on the social landscape but the stalking and subsequent murder of the actress Rebecca Schaeffer by an obsessed fan in 1989 triggered its entry into the public imagination. In the early 1990s there was a tenfold increase in media coverage of stalking and the name itself became part of popular culture. Los Angeles became known as the stalking capital of the world. Between 1992 and 1995 anti-stalking laws were passed in forty-nine states leading to numerous articles in newspapers as well as law journals. About 200,000 stalking cases were reported each year, according to victim rights organisations.

It was not long before stalking became a public issue in the UK. High-profile cases and publicity led to a widespread view that existing laws were inadequate to deal with the problem and finally resulted in anti-stalking legislation in the form of the 1997 Protection from Harassment Act, making it an offence in criminal and civil law to harass another person. It was officially recognised that stalkers can have a devastating effect on the lives of their victims and that it is an oppressive behaviour that no society can tolerate.

According to NASH, the UK National Anti-Stalking and Harassment Campaign, about 7,000 victims telephoned its help-line between January 1994 and November 1995, though there are no reliable statistics beyond that. Most stalkers are men and most victims of stalking are women. According to NASH, 95 per cent of those who called its help-line were women. In America it is believed that at least half the women who leave violent relationships are subsequently followed and threatened by their abusers. As many as 90 per cent of women killed by former partners were stalked before the murder occurred. And it is estimated that about 5 per cent of women in the general population will be victims of stalking at some time in their lives.

In the 1990s a scientific literature developed analysing the origins and nature of stalking. What is usually emphasised is the diversity of types, motives and methods. Stalking is often divided according to the psychological profile of the stalker: for example, 'erotomania' where the stalker has the erotic delusion that he is loved by his victim; 'borderline erotomania' where the stalker knows that the victim does not return his intense emotional feelings; 'former intimates' where the stalker did have a relationship with his victim but refuses to accept their estrangement; and 'sociopaths' where the stalker is a serial murderer or rapist who stalks his victim before committing violence (though often not with the intent of making his surveillance known). The stalker may be an obsessed fan, a separated lover, a rejected suitor, a patient or student harbouring erotic desires for an authority figure, a resentful ex-employee or even a complete stranger selecting an anonymous target.

Motives for stalking are seen within this literature as equally diverse: they range from forcing the victim to recognise that she has a relationship with or even loves the stalker, to taking revenge for a relationship that has broken down or for a suit that has been rejected, to punishing an authority figure or idol who has failed to live up to his or her status, to some more generic notion of securing justice in return for wrongs previously inflicted. Stalking is often most virulent when the stalker believes that he himself has been persecuted by his victim.

The methods employed by stalkers are similarly diverse. They may include actions which are in themselves unlawful, like obscene phone calls, abusive language, threats, property damage and violence. But often they centre around actions which seem at first sight to be innocuous, routine, harmless and lawful – for example, the stalker may follow his victim down a street, send her flowers, watch her home or place of work, or simply make his presence felt. In many cases stalking escalates from less nocuous acts like sending flowers to a woman who has made it clear that she does not want them, to more menacing acts like sending a wreath. The harm which the stalker commits is that of causing his victim distress, anxiety, alarm or even terror through the sheer, oppressive persistence of his unwanted presence. This may be inflicted on the victim without her consent over a period of many years.

I have been stalked since November 1993 and it is not over yet. One peculiarity of my case is that I am a man and my stalker is a woman; another is that the stalker has had the active support of her husband. The stalker, whom I shall call Mrs M in this memoir, was originally a student of mine. I am an academic at the University of Warwick and we met when she took my course on the Sociology of the Modern State. At the time of writing this memoir the stalking has gone on for three and a half years. In contrast to some cases of stalking, my story has involved neither direct acts of violence nor explicit threats of violence and I am still here to tell the tale. It is not an extreme instance. And yet both in its mildness and in its peculiarities, this story reveals secrets not only about stalking itself but more generally about how oppressive, even persecutory, relations between individuals can become in our times and how difficult it is to find ways of living through them.

My stalker is on the surface an ordinary, unremarkable woman. She is in her mid- to late forties, works as a part-time word-processing operator, is married to a machinist in an engineering factory, and is the mother of three grown-up daughters. With little education behind her she took a sociology A level at a local College of Further Education and did well to get a place on a part-time degree programme at the University of Warwick. Her achievement was all the more considerable in that she had long been looking after a sick mother and a sick daughter. Mrs M lives with her family in a detached, modern house in a part of Coventry called Tile Hill, a respectable working-class area not far from the university. In her appearance she seems to aspire to old-fashioned respectability: she is fairly tall, of average weight, tries to dress smartly, and has dyed her hair red. She used to be recognisable by her rather striking royal blue coat. Her husband was shorter and squatter; he didn't say much and when he spoke he did so with pugnacious difficulty. It took me a long while to see how alike they looked.

Throughout this whole affair Mrs M has presented herself as a commoner fighting for her rights against the forces of privilege, as a woman fighting for justice against man's abuse of power, and as a good Christian fighting for decency against sexual misconduct and immorality.

I have not been a stranger to privilege. When this stalking started, I was a Senior Lecturer in the Sociology Department of Warwick University. Now I am what is known as a Reader (a fairly senior position in the academic hierarchy). The university to which I 'belong' is a large and wealthy institution located on the edges of Coventry. It offers little sense of inner-city life in its ever-expanding campus, its modern buildings, well-manicured lawns and surrounding rusticity. I have an office to myself – with my own telephone, desk, computer and books – and my window (during most of the time that I have been stalked) overlooked a large courtyard whose summer walkways are covered in hanging clumps of purple wisteria. I have been at the university for many years and my job is secure. During the stalking my department moved to a new building whose isolated and spare architecture was the price we paid for more space.

I was born into a well-to-do, north-west London, Jewish family. I went to a public school, entered Oxford as a Classics scholar and then switched to Politics, Philosophy and Economics. After graduating in 1967 I went off to study sociology at Columbia University in New York. There I was left gasping at the chasm between American democratic values and the brute violence of its war in Vietnam and immediately joined the anti-war movement. I became a student radical, participated in this culture and experienced first-hand that 'devaluation of all values' which I subsequently read about in books. Later I found an interesting job teaching at Brooklyn College, City University of New York, until in 1973 I returned to England. There I was influenced by Marxism, joined various socialist organisations and have stayed ever since at Warwick.

My father died in 1981. Despite many illnesses my mother lived to a good old age until she died in 1994. My elder brother and I, despite many differences of politics and lifestyle (he works in the City and prefers the Tories), have become close. Around the time my father died, I settled down with my partner. We had a daughter in 1986 but our relationship broke up painfully in 1992 – a year before the stalking began. The 'divorce' was the result of many problems, not least those of perceived and real inequality and the aftermath was difficult.

By the time the stalking began, I was living alone in a bungalow in Leamington Spa. Situated on an estate built in the 1960s and favoured by retired couples, it is functional and bright, with picture windows to the front into which passers-by can look if they feel like it, a neglectfully wild garden surrounded by many different hedges, and a setting which compensates for its architectural limitations. The common across the road, known as the Comyn, is a lush meadow on which are scattered horse chestnuts, oaks, hawthorns and beech. Behind it are thick woods (now an Area of Natural Beauty) going steeply down to the River Leam. The road leads to a pub, a leisure centre, where I often swim in the morning before work, playing fields and a golf course. There it ends.

I moved into my bungalow ten months after I separated from my partner, attracted by its pristine lack of memory, its closeness to the swimming pool and its rustic ambience. Most important, my young daughter lives nearby and visits a lot but never enough. Often I have friends calling and thanks to my daughter I acquired a shaggy mutt of a dog called Fudge.

At least four days a week during term-time I travel the nine miles between my home and university by car. At the university I usually park my car in a multi-storey car park in the middle of the campus and from there I walk a few minutes either to my office or to the Arts Centre coffee bar or straight to a lecture theatre. For the rest of my work-time I stay at home writing or go away to conferences and research visits. Like most academics I work hard but also have the benefit of flexible hours, considerable autonomy and work that I am committed to.

I can obviously say much more about myself than about Mrs M but beneath the label of 'stalking' I recognised a social conflict between a man and a woman, privilege and underprivilege, educational advantage and disadvantage, radicalism and respectability and even perhaps Jewishness and Christianity.

I have rarely 'felt' the privilege which I undoubtedly have. One reason for this is that I have suffered as long as I can remember from a form of bad health which often makes it physically difficult for me to speak and which leaves me feeling on the outside of every inside: never quite belonging to any social grouping and never quite sure if the future will have any resemblance to the past.

Another is that a sense of reason does not come easily to me and when it does it slips away unnoticed in the face of more powerful forces. I do not think that these afflictions are special – we all, as it is said, have our crosses to bear – but they are strong enough to keep me on my toes.

I am a socialist and should like to think that my socialism – though less active than it used to be, less wedded to any 'ism', even that of the social, and less sure that those who are injured in life will not simply injure back – is still able to recognise that social relations are not fixed and that the debilitating consequences of class inequality are not an inescapable part of the human condition. The fact that deprivation and a legitimate sense of injustice may sometimes lead to madness and malice rather than to enlightenment and emancipation, and the fact that socialists may not live up to their principles, seem to me to be no reason to abandon the house of socialism. Rather I should like to open it up to real human beings.

Stalking is a struggle for recognition between the stalker and myself, mediated by institutions, the law and other individuals. While Mrs M claimed justice on her side, I claimed innocence. Neither of these simple claims ever seemed quite adequate to capture the burden of events. I found dreadfully impressive the sense of 'absolute right' that my stalker maintained and the persistence with which she pursued her cause to the end – even at the expense of her own possible self-destruction. I often felt that I was being pursued by an ancient Fury intent on punishing me for injuries done or imagined. Her invocation of 'ancient laws' had little in common with

8

modern conceptions of the democratisation of public and private life. It reminded me rather of how the name of 'right' may be invoked to justify the persecution of other human beings – not just the so-called 'old rights' which legitimise traditional hierarchies but also those new rights of the New Right which express for the 1990s the resentment of the 'mass man', shorn of social connections, against the institutions and representatives of civil society.

As for my own claims to innocence, I am reminded of a passage from Kafka's *Trial* where the painter Titorelli said: 'If you are innocent, then the matter is quite simple.' K replied, 'My innocence doesn't make the matter any simpler.' This is my experience too.

The first five parts of this memoir are written in a style of pure narration. They recount from my point of view 'what happened' and address in a realistic mode my experience of being stalked. The final two parts are more reflective and address directly the forms and categories of my own experience. I would have liked to merge them more but the separation itself reflects what happened in my own mind. As I look upon this individual who was 'being stalked', I see someone at first in hiding whose mode of survival was through the denial of effect and affect and who dissolved himself into the detached narrative voice of one undisturbed by the vicissitudes of life. Later I see the traces of one prepared to emerge in his own way and his own time, whose response to the grindingly repetitive routines of being stalked was more than to mimic grinding repetition.

I am called by the media and the law the 'victim' but I balk at the pathos and passivity of this label and wish to swim against the current that places the voice of the victim too close to the vortex of truth and justice. A voice, yes, but not new privilege. A victim is not just a victim and my voice is already *my* voice. The passive tense of the title *being stalked* concealed the active presence of what the sociologist Erving Goffman would have called *doing being stalked*. It is an act of 'doing' with its own ways of experiencing and expressing events, its own drives, motives and ends.

1
The Accusation

How does stalking begin? I cannot answer this question in general but in my case it began with an accusation. Back in November 1993.

It was her anger that first drew Mrs M to my attention. I saw in it a quality of unforgiving self-righteousness which I associated with an earlier, less reflexive age and more vaguely with my mother. The anger was directed at another student whose failure to do the work asked of her compelled Mrs M to present alone her thoughts on 'Marx's theory of the state'. When her indignation boiled over at the end of the seminar, I suggested that we discuss the matter some other time. On the following Monday morning she came to my office where I advised her to focus on her own studies rather than the shortcomings of other students. We talked about the course for a few minutes until there was a knock at the door. At this point Mrs M left.

It seemed to me to be an unremarkable encounter but Mrs M's perception of it proved very different. On Wednesday evening at 8.30, at the end of another late-finishing seminar, Mrs M asked to see me alone in my office. Resisting the siren calls of whisky and TV football, I agreed. Once inside, she passed me a folded sheet of paper on which was typed a message. It took me some time to grasp its meaning but I got there in the end: cryptically but definitively it contained the charge that I had sexually propositioned her during that previous encounter in my office. I handed her back the note.

She said, 'You are not trying to deny it, are you, Dr Fine?' I did deny it, guessing at what the 'it' was. 'Are you calling me a liar, Dr Fine?' she said next. There was something about the way she spoke the words 'Dr Fine' that I found as disturbing as the substance of the accusation – perhaps it was because most students called me by my first name. I said I wasn't accusing her of anything but that she must have been mistaken. She insisted: 'I do not imagine things and I am not neurotic.' I assured her I wasn't saying that she imagined things nor that she was neurotic, only that she was wrong. She persisted: 'I have a perfect memory for detail, so why don't you just admit it and apologise?' I doubtless looked as confused as I felt. She became all the more adamant. She said she was a respectable mother of three daughters, that she had been happily married for twenty years, that she had worked for the police, that men had never bothered her before, that she had been looking after her ailing mother and that other students needed to be protected. There was one last unveiled threat before I asked her to leave my office: 'You could lose your job over this, you know, Dr Fine.' I felt I was in the presence of a hermetic mind that had closed the gates to counter-argument.

From that moment on Mrs M regularly repeated and elaborated her charge. The gap between my lecture which finished at seven o'clock, and the seminar which started a few minutes later, was her moment of opportunity to engage me in front of other students. She complained that I had given her headaches and that she couldn't concentrate on her work because of them; I felt she was giving me a headache. She accused me of discriminating against her 'because of what happened'; I tried to reassure her that she would be treated in a normal, professional way. Once she said with real anguish and fury, 'You are destroying my life, Dr Fine.' I said I neither wanted to nor could do that. She told me that other students had noticed I had been looking at her in peculiar ways and that she had informed them of my 'sexual advances'. Later I learnt that Mrs M had also sent to their home addresses a 'questionnaire' which contained questions like:

'Did you notice Dr Fine look at Mrs M for longer
   periods than normal?'
'Did you see Dr Fine stand behind Mrs M at all
   during seminars?'
'Did you see Dr Fine sit next to her at all?'
'Did you see him sit opposite her?'
'If you sat near Mrs M, did you notice Dr Fine
   looking more than usual in that direction?'
'Did you observe anything between them at all?'
'Did you believe that they had "something going
   on?"'

She wrote to one of the students asking her to verify the 'incidents' between Mrs M and myself which she had observed. During lectures and seminars she usually said nothing but looked angry and distraught. In one seminar she passed me an open note, via the hands of half the class, demanding to see me on an urgent and private matter. It turned out she wanted to discuss her essay. Often she waited near my office door, either saying nothing or insistent that I talk to her alone in my room.

She threatened to report me to the university for 'unprofessional conduct' and raise it in front of other students. When I tried to dissuade her, she said that she might not be able to stop herself. Her basic charge was that I not only propositioned her on that fateful occasion in my office but was continuing to proposition her in everyday encounters.

I am sure that my anxiety in Mrs M's presence showed. I kept trying to avoid her and heard her shouting 'You don't have to run away from me, Dr Fine', as I dashed upstairs and she followed. I was agitated, though not overwhelmed, by her allegations and involvement of other students. From time to time I made warning noises that I would report her if she continued to harass me, but for a long time I sought to persude her that her beliefs were mistaken and that she should turn back to her studies. She sometimes seemed assuaged by these discussions but not for long. She would return a few days later laden with the weight of new charges.

I was upset by these accusations and talked about my difficulties with a few friends and colleagues, including the head of my department, Professor Jim Beckford. He advised me to report Mrs M formally to the university but at first I declined this advice, thinking I could manage the situation myself. I have an entrenched antipathy to reporting anyone to authority. In early March 1994, however, at the urging of Jim Beckford, I dictated a letter to Helen Davis, the lecturer responsible for part-time students. I wrote that Mrs M had levelled a series of 'extraordinary accusations' against me – that I was making advances towards her, looking at her in funny ways and making personal comments – and that I had told her it was 'entirely imaginary' on her part. Since then, I wrote, she persistently pestered me, accused me of lying, and issued threats. I did not send this letter but had it filed with our departmental secretary. When about a month later I heard that Mrs M had gone (with one of her daughters) to see Jim Beckford and Helen Davis to inform them of her allegations, I finally sent the letter with a covering note to explain why I hadn't sent it before. 'I was hoping to handle the situation without official contact,' I said, without calling for any official intervention.

In the summer term of 1994 Mrs M came to all my revision seminars, those for full-time as well as part-time students, and tried to insist on her right to tape-record them. Some of the other students complained and by this time I was exasperated by her behaviour. I refused to talk to her any more except in class and was simply looking forward to the end of the teaching year in the hope that it would mark the end of this unhappy acquaintance. It was not to be. In June 1994 I learnt that Mrs M had made a formal complaint of sexual harassment and had sent a 27-page document detailing the allegations. An Investigating Committee was established to decide whether there was a case to answer. This was my first step into that world of 'committees' and 'courts' that were to become a major part of my life for the next three years.

Before seeing Mrs M's affidavit, I was asked to outline the nature of my dealings with her and offer any other comments. I said what I felt: that sexual harassment is a serious offence and has to be dealt with seriously, but in this particular case I denied any wrongdoing on my part. I said it was she who had harassed and threatened me and declared my innocence. I was to some extent looking forward to airing this musty matter in public, but being accused of sexual harassment in front of my colleagues caused me real anxiety. I never did have faith in the dictum that if you've done nothing wrong, you have nothing to fear.

In her affidavit Mrs M was able to spell out in detail her own view of what had happened. She wrote how on that first occasion in my office 'a distinct sexual advance was made' and that she was sure I was 'thinking of sex' and 'wanted sex then and there'. The general thread that ran all the way through the 27 pages concerned how I looked at her and how she experienced my looking. It was about what went out from my eyes – how they glanced, stared, penetrated, pierced, suggested, undressed, propositioned and terrified – and how she received these looks. She saw them basically as proffering a sexualised and objectifying male gaze.

The phraseology Mrs M used in her covering letter – that I looked at her with 'hard penetrating stares' and 'sexually suggestive ones' – set the scene for the rest. Scattered around the text were statements such as the following:

'his constant fixed stares unnerved me and gave me an uneasy feeling';

'he fixed on me with a hard stare which almost seemed to pierce into me. It made me feel shaky and nervous';

'he was looking discreetly at the back of me – looking me up and down ... he took into view the whole of the front of me';

'he got right up to me; his head and face

16

fractionally off my bust and then he looked up at
me; and deeply into my eyes';
'he had invaded my personal space ... it had
sexual significance';
'he was looking at me hard ... he looked at my
legs';
'he looked at me really examining every detail ... I
felt naked ... he was obviously looking at my
body and thinking of sex ... He moved his eyes
to my bust again ...'

I was struck by her use of the word 'bust', which I had
not heard outside the context of lingerie and sculpture
for a long time. To me it spoke of embarrassment at the
sound of 'breasts' and had the connotation of something
undivided, matronly and unsexed. More importantly, I
interrogated myself as to what I had done to provoke
these comments.

The affidavit often read like an old-fashioned romance
in which the male hero fixes on the heroine 'with a hard
stare which almost seemed to pierce into her'. Mrs M
wrote that I treated her as a 'sexual object', but according
to her own account on every occasion except the first she
was the one who sought appointments with me, came to
my door, followed me upstairs, waited outside my
lecture room, asked whether there was something about
her which attracted me and told me not to avoid her.
There was nothing passive about her. In one passage, for
example, she wrote:

I edged up to him but he reacted quickly – dropped
his eyes looking at my bust again and thumped his
hands hard down on the table as if trying to stop

himself from touching me. This frightened me and I remained riveted to the spot. He said that I should not go to his room again but would not explain why. Eventually, I said 'Now let's get this straight you don't want me to come to your room again in case you say something we both know you've said but you may wish to deny later? Is that right?' 'Yes,' he said with a laugh. He said, 'Can't you treat it as a misunderstanding?' 'Sorry,' I said, 'Can't do that.'

My denials of sexual interest were not accepted. When my eyes looked down, it was to look at her breasts. When I thumped my hands on the table in exasperation, it was to stop myself from touching her. When I refused to talk, it was to dismiss her 'like a schoolgirl'. When I asked a secretary to interrupt an encounter between us, it was a conspiracy lest we be found 'in a compromising position'. She seemed as infuriated by my rejections, indifference, avoidance and flight as she was by the alleged sexual advances:

I told him if he stared at me again or annoyed me for instance running away from me I would stand up, no matter where I was with no matter how many people around, whether it was the lecture, seminar or whatever and tell everyone what he had done and said to me ... He said, 'If that's a threat then I don't want you on my course.' I said, 'It's not a threat it is what I am capable of if you continue to annoy me.'

What annoyed her was my 'whole attitude' (which she described as 'bright and perky'), as well as my advice that she should study (and that's all) and my refusal to see her alone in my office. Indifference seemed as maddening as appetite, disregard as unnerving as *le regard*.

I thought that Mrs M craved a recognition on my part of my desire for her and that she was looking every-where for signs of its truth – especially in eye contact and the avoidance of eye contact.

> He was obviously aware that I was avoiding his eyes and did the same. This I found strange – unless I really was right – I still had doubts. He walked to the blackboard and did some writing and then stood behind me. P—— caught my eye and nodded in his direction indicating that he was looking at me. When I looked around he looked down. Strange behaviour for a lecturer I thought.

Eye contact is always a complex moment of interaction: for Mrs M it involved not only my looking at her and her awareness of being looked at, but also my awareness of her awareness that I was watching her. 'I think he realised that I had noticed him watching me,' she wrote with indicative complexity. If I tried to hide looking at her or looked away, she wrote, my devious methods didn't fool her for a moment. As for myself, not knowing whether in seminars to look at her or not to look at her, had certainly become a self-conscious embarrassment.

It was important to Mrs M that other people corrobo-rated her version of events, but she seemed to permit 'other people' no independent existence outside her own mind. She invoked the agreement of others with her definition of the situation but did little to substantiate it in terms of what they had to say. For example, she wrote:

When I entered the lecture room everyone seemed of the opinion that I had just come from his room (as though they also had noticed how he was with me) but in actual fact I had been late leaving work ... Sue came in later than me and I asked her if she had just been to his room. From this people who were seated nearby me realised that I could not have been in his room and so all was well again.

The scene took place exclusively in the head of the writer, or at least there was no evidence to the contrary. Elsewhere she wrote of how the other students

were informed by me that I had gone to see him the previous week in his room and only discussed work nothing more (although more was inferred jokingly by them at first). I had to clear my reputation.

She asked other students whether they had 'problems' with me and whether they too received 'the special treatment' in my room, and she told them that I discriminated against her in marking her essay. But all this was reported as if her telling the story was identical to its endorsement. In fact, none of the other students backed her and when several of them wrote to the head of department offering to give evidence on my behalf, Mrs M explained this away as the students' fear of challenging authority. I think she constructed what she wanted to hear. For instance, she claimed that Jim Beckford 'half-nodded' when she told her story, 'apologised' for my behaviour and said he could not replace me 'due to a shortage of staff'. Jim said that none of this was true.

It seemed to me that Mrs M attributed to my actions as a teacher an excess of meaning which always centred on herself. For instance, she wrote that I once arrived at my lecture on time (a cruel blow!) to prove that I was not lying to her, or that I deliberately waited for her to arrive before starting a lecture to show that I wanted her to be there, or that I referred to her as 'Elaine' (which was not her name) as a purposeful slip of the tongue in order to make out to other students that I didn't know her well. She combined this overloading of significance with repeated denials that she was over-sensitive or neurotic or imagining things – or indeed that she had any feelings whatsoever for me 'except to recapture her good name, return to study, receive an apology' and have some form of record made against me. She affirmed her own respectability as a 'devoted mother and faithful wife', while in my smallest gesture, glance or slip of the tongue she read the marks of a 'guilty man'.

I had to brace myself to read Mrs M's affidavit. I could scarcely believe that she saw our encounters in the way she did, but I did not doubt her conviction. I discussed it with friends and then, mainly with a view to rebutting it, I wrote to the Investigating Committee that the allegations were 'a piece of nonsense' and that there was not a shred of evidence to support her claims. I said that the document showed clearly that Mrs M was the one who had done the harassing and that I had showed forbearance in trying to help her. I said the way in which she interpreted innocent acts and gestures as if they were sexual and suggestive was entirely subjective and that her capacity for fabrication was evident in the difference between her account of events and that of reliable third parties. I said that what she omitted from her document

– like her 'questionnaire' and letter to the other students – was as significant as what she included. And finally I said that the document itself was evidence of her obsessive sexual interest in me despite my repeated denials of interest in her. I asked the committee to absolve me, to write to students and staff to whom Mrs M had distributed her letters to clear my name, and to initiate a review of Mrs M's own standing as a student.

Beneath the surface of these claims and counter-claims, however, I was not unaffected by the deep sense of powerlessness, injustice and repressed sexual desire that I read in Mrs M's words. It seemed to me that it was in its own way a painful record of what is so often missing in our lives. The ubiquity of the themes of sex, power and justice within the text expressed something important and true for me: that they are all essential ingredients of a good life and that their lack is unbearable. We are sometimes told that on this earth we *can* or even *should* live without sex, power and justice in anticipation of acquiring them in the world to come, but can we have a *good* life without them? I do not think so. Their absence will somehow be felt and expressed. I think that Mrs M was ashamed of these natural inclinations and instinctively sought a cause for her suffering in the shape of someone to blame. That someone was me.

Mrs M was unshakeable in her belief that she had been wronged. This conviction gave her an explanation for her own suffering and a justification for her relentless pursuit of 'justice'. Confronted by this attribution of blame, I presented myself as the innocent victim and her as the guilty perpetrator. I don't think that either of us doubted for a moment the truth of our claims.

After all the threats, lies and innuendoes it came as a relief to offer my story in public – even as the accused. I was questioned in detail about what happened on that fateful occasion in my office and on my subsequent behaviour towards Mrs M. The questioning was, as it should be, thorough and professional: Had I propositioned her? Did I look at her in suggestive ways? Did I look at her breasts? Had I approached her in my office? How far was my seat from hers? Was there a table between myself and her? Was the door closed? Who knocked on the door? The questions entered into the nitty-gritty of teaching space and time and I answered them as best I could. I felt very divided: on the one hand, reasonably confident that the committee would be impressed by the emptiness of her allegations; on the other hand, extremely uncomfortable at being the target of all these potentially damaging questions.

Though I didn't know it at the time, my case was helped by two students who wrote to the committee to say that they had seen nothing wrong in my behaviour. One of them included a letter that she had received from Mrs M in which she had written that:

> a number of incidents occurred between myself and Dr Fine. I believe some were observed by you personally. I make specific reference to an instance when he stood behind me and you indicated he was looking at me. When I turned around he looked away.

The student said there was nothing in my manner to suggest I was looking at Mrs M – I was merely answering a question. Mrs M asked her to verify how 'strange' my behaviour was during her seminar on feminism: 'He did not wish to be in the room. He would not listen to any argument.' The student said she did not give a presentation on feminism but on 'women's exclusion from civil society' and that she did not know what Mrs M meant about my not listening to any arguments. Mrs M wrote that she heard this student say out loud that 'there was something going on between us'; the student said she had no recollection of saying this. The two students volunteered to give oral evidence on my behalf, but I don't know if they did. Jim Beckford also wrote to the committee saying that my teaching received 'nothing but praise' from the students and that his impression of Mrs M was that she was 'deeply confused, defensive and distressed'. He said that there was no evidence to support her claim that I tried to seduce and then conspire against her, but there was corroborated evidence of her aggressiveness towards fellow-students.

The committee decided that the complaint against me was unfounded. In mid-July 1994, some eight months after first being accused by Mrs M of propositioning her, I was informed of the committee's conclusions:

The interpretations placed upon events by Mrs M were not supported by the evidence ... and depended entirely on Mrs M's perception of events which did not appear to the Committee to be reasonable ... you have conducted yourself in a fully professional manner towards Mrs M ... despite the considerable difficulties which arose between you and Mrs M ... The Vice-Chancellor has approved the recommendation of the Committee that Mrs M be cautioned ... against any repetition of the allegations she has made against you. I will be writing to those members of academic staff who have been involved in this matter and to those students who have received question-naires and letters from Mrs M to inform them that the matter has been fully investigated and that there is no foundation in the allegations which have been made against you.

I was enormously relieved by the outcome. As far as I was concerned, that was the end of an unpleasant episode in my life and work. In the summer vacation I took myself off to breathe some fresh, French mountain air in the hope and expectation that I would have no further dealings with Mrs M. Again this was to prove wrong.

Mrs M clearly made known her belief that the decision of the committee was unjust. She claimed that her com-plaint had been heard under the wrong statute – one which referred to 'conduct of an immoral, scandalous or disgraceful nature incompatible with the duties of office' – and that this alone accounted for my exoneration. I was never clear what the right statute would have been except that it would not have involved the loss of my job. With an air of conciliation she wrote:

I never intended that Dr Fine's job should be in jeopardy at all ... only to highlight a problem and report his actions toward me ... He never did deserve to lose his job for what happened between us ... I am telling the truth about what did happen. I did not want Dr Fine penalised at all just noticed. In this respect my complaint has been successful ... I would

also like to thank you for notifying everyone who I
sent letters and questionnaires to, of the outcome. Of
course, they already were well aware that I could not
win the case and the reasons for my going ahead ... I
am aware my decision to make the matter formal has
offended many Academic members of staff and for
this I humbly apologise ...

She maintained, however, that she had told the truth and
had gone ahead 'for the principle of the matter' (17 July
1994).

Soon her position hardened. She secretly tape-
recorded a meeting with Professor Duke and Cathy
Charlton, the chair and secretary of the Investigating
Committee, in which she intimated that no justice could
be expected from a university body dedicated to protecting its own: 'It is not going to be a total surprise that I
have not won the case because I was already well aware
of the fact that I wouldn't win.' When Professor Duke
rejected the innuendo, pointing out that the result was an
open question until the end of the proceeding, Mrs M
immediately turned disagreement into a challenge to her
veracity: 'I cannot possibly accept that you say that I am
lying.' To Professor Duke's comment that I had conducted myself in a fully professional manner, she added:
'except in his room'. When Professor Duke said that she
had been cautioned not to repeat the allegations, she
said, 'I can't prove it. That's the problem, I can't prove it
... it is absolutely ridiculous to caution me. I am grown
up enough ... There is no point in my lying. What
happened, happened ... I just tried to get the truth,
that's all.' When Professor Duke put it to her that her
experience was one of 'total conviction' – the belief that

one's perceptions are absolutely right even when they are not – neither she nor her husband could accept that interpretation. They were not to be budged from their persuasion that an injustice had been committed, not just by me but now also by the university.

At the same time Mrs M also began battling with the university over a fail-mark in another course and another department. I found it a bit odd because she only failed the examination and not the course as a whole, so the mark would make no substantial difference to her degree. But the real point was that she attributed her failure to my influence and to the effects of her allegation. She thought that the university was discriminating against her because she had taken action against one of its members. She involved her local MP, John Butcher, who asked the university to provide a copy of her examination paper for 'independent scrutiny'. The university refused, saying it was satisfied that the mark had been properly awarded. Soon after this she made a formal complaint and John Butcher arranged a meeting with the registrar 'to ensure that fair play was observed'. At the meeting Mrs M questioned the professional competence of the head of the Department of Applied Social Studies, Professor Hilary Graham (who was also one of the markers), called the external examiner 'biased' and claimed that 'colleagues all stood together'. Supported by John Butcher, she again demanded that an independent examiner be brought in to review the paper: when this was again refused, she said she was not surprised, given that 'colleagues back each other up'. Her resentment towards me was fused with an ever firmer conviction that no justice could be secured through an institution of privilege like the university.

In January 1995 Mrs M appealed the decision of the Investigating Committee and the failed examination mark to the Lord Chancellor's Department. According to regal prerogative the Lord Chancellor acted on behalf of the Queen as the 'Visitor' to the university and in this capacity served as a court of final appeal. In other words, Mrs M went to the top. In her many letters to the Lord Chancellor, copies of which I later saw in the court records, she connected her fail-mark closely with her complaint against me. She said that Rose Watson, the tutor in the course she failed, had her office just a few doors away from mine and that she even came to my lectures. In every silence or gesture of Dr Watson she found signs of either conspiracy or corroboration:

> Dr Watson said at first she did not know of the complaint I had made about Dr Fine. When I said, 'I think you know', she said she had heard rumours ... she said she was 'Sorry that our friend has been pestering you'. So she did know – why pretend not to? ... she said 'shut the door if you are going to say anything'. I told her that I would be lucky to get a 3.3 from the Sociology Department after making my complaint and she nodded in agreement.

Mrs M said that the senior tutor, Tom Stone, who was in charge of student welfare, had admitted before a witness that the mark was a 'shut-up mark', but told her to accept it if she wanted a degree at Warwick. After a heated argument, she said, he refused to represent her. Quoting a secretly tape-recorded conversation, she said that Professor Graham could not explain the fail-mark, 'constantly shifted her argument' and could not justify calling Mrs M's paper 'seriously muddled'. She alleged collusion between the external examiner, the internal markers and myself: 'they are hardly impartial colleagues', and questioned the motivation behind the university's decision not to release her examination script:

> The truth is that you dare not release that work, because you know very well it would be proof positive that procedures and regulations have not been followed. It is the only way I can prove it. There is no way you are going to give me that ...

The registrar wrote to the Lord Chancellor that these allegations were 'defamatory ... and wholly unsupported by the facts of the case'.

Asked by the Lord Chancellor whether she wished to pursue her complaint of sexual harassment, she expressed her disapproval of the result 'as if I was the guilty person and yet verbally neither lying nor imagining things', but decided not to pursue the complaint since 'no student will come forward to support me ... because they are all protecting their degrees'. To ensure her complaint went to the highest authority, Mrs M sent a copy to the Queen at Buckingham Palace, whose officer replied that the Lord Chancellor acts on the Queen's behalf. So she wrote once again to him:

> I am a 48 year old woman, married for 23 years with three daughters, who has strong moral beliefs. I do not believe it is fair that I am victimised because of them. I DID NOT FAIL THAT EXAMINATION ... I remain an extremely disgruntled fee-paying ... student ... who has tried to obtain an education for herself after

nursing her sick mother for years and devoting herself to her family . . . I am powerless without your help . . .

She presented herself as a decent woman of strong moral beliefs who was a victim of injustice. In order to restore the moral order, she appealed to the highest authority in the land, the Queen, and began to take justice into her own hands. In the most literal sense, it was to be an eye for an eye.

One swallow does not make a summer. One false accusation of sexual harassment does not make the charge itself into an enemy. No general conclusions can be drawn from a single case. I do not wish this episode to be read like David Mamet's play *Oleanna*, where Carol, the student, accuses John, the lecturer, of attempted rape 'according to the law' on the grounds that he pressed his body into her as she was leaving his office. Mamet makes her say that 'My Group has told your lawyer that we may pursue criminal charges' and that John must not call his wife 'baby'. Here the last word is given unequivocally to John: 'You think that you can come in here with your political correctness and destroy my life?' We are invited to identify with him when he picks up a chair, raises it above his head and advances on her shouting: 'I wouldn't touch you with a ten-foot pole. You little *cunt* . . .', and when she cowers on the floor below him. Such misogyny is as superficial and self-righteous as it is bitter.

What lay behind Mrs M's perceptions? Could it be that she simply misread my open manner as a sexual proposition because of the difference between the complex norms of everyday university life – where students call me Robert and not Dr Fine but where the switch from formality to informality and back again is a matter of ongoing renegotiation – and the more conventional norms to which she was possibly accustomed? The university is not a safe world, its boundaries are inherently unclear and traditional rules of 'knowing your place' lose their self-evidence. In this setting there are no well-defined signs and no clear conventions concerning what constitutes a legitimate interest in another. It is a 'risk society' in which judgement is reflective rather than determinate, a question less of applying rules to concrete situations than of groping for rules in particular cases.

One official way of dealing with the risks posed by this environment is to construct seemingly absolute legal prohibitions – for instance, that a teacher will never in any circumstances proposition a student. Or we may follow the path which I think Mrs M took, and turn any informality or dropping of the professional mask into a sign of transgression. Faced with the contingency of interpersonal relations in this complex setting and with the difficulty of approaching other adults as emotional equals, our response may be to withdraw into an absolute normative order. Confronted by the open-textured relations of university life, we may submerge our self-identity in fixed rules and recognise our own lack of autonomy only by resenting it in others. Where freedom to choose is an impossible burden, anxiety is the demon which makes us surrender the faculty of critical, reflective judgement in exchange for unconditioned rules and a single, overarching authority.

When we are overwhelmed by a sense of our own powerlessness, what is to stop us dealing with it through fantasies of dominance in which we orchestrate the world like a puppeteer? When we are overwhelmed by a sense of deep injustice, why should we not imagine that everything can be put right by an alliance of the highest law and our lowliest selves? When we are overwhelmed by our own lack of joy and pleasure, is there not an inclination to turn necessity into virtue and do anything to discredit the pleasure of others? It was somewhere in this night-world of the imagination that I traced the path that was to lead from accusation to stalking.

2
The Stalking, 1994–5

What I later learnt to call stalking began in September 1994. One day I arrived home to find a car parked opposite my house. Mrs M was in the passenger seat and next to her was a man whom I then thought and later knew to be her husband – they watched me while I walked my dog on the common and watched my house after I returned. I wrote to Chris Duke, the chair of the Investigating Committee, to express my 'displeasure and unease'. It was unacceptable, I said, for any student to loiter outside a staff member's home but in this case it was absolutely unacceptable. My letter was passed to Jim Rushton, the university's deputy registrar, who wrote to Mrs M asking to see her.

Mrs M's reply was written in mock and mocking legalese. She had checked with Coventry police to confirm that, providing she caused no obstruction, contravened no road sign and had the correct documents, no offence had been committed. The public highway, she said, gives free access to every vehicle, parked or otherwise. A vehicle can remain unattended for 21 days without notice before being removed. A passenger (her husband was driving) cannot be held responsible for the destination of a vehicle. She insisted that the university had no jurisdiction over what she did during her leisure time – particularly since the area in question lay outside the campus. Referring all future correspondence to her solicitor, she declared that she was more concerned with her failed examination mark than with 'listening to gossip on matters which are beyond the scope of the University's powers'.

To a further letter, this time from the registrar of the university, Mike Shattock, Mrs M replied that she had never been parked outside my front *door* (correct – she had been opposite my front *window*), insisted she would use the 'amenities' in my area as she wished, complained that the registrar's letter sounded 'like an accusation' and impugned my motive for raising the issue:

> If Dr Fine wishes to assume that any vehicle containing my person is parked in the vicinity purely to intimidate or harass him, then there is nothing I can say to convince you otherwise. Could it be a question of guilt I wonder?

Outside the university, she insisted, she was a 'private citizen using public amenities'. She strongly contested the university's right to 'dictate' what she could or could not do in her own time.

Mrs M always maintained a libertarian insistence on her rights: the right to walk on public land, to use public amenities and indeed to do whatever she wanted within the bounds of the law, regardless of how uncomfortable or distressing or alarming I found her behaviour. I recognised that this argument was not easily dismissed and my confrontation with it was to recur throughout the whole period of my being stalked. At the same time Mrs M also prided herself on her good relations with authority. In particular, she said she had worked alongside the police for several years and that 'after a very close relative died under tragic circumstances ... the Police Officers who had worked alongside this relative honoured the funeral with their presence in large numbers and with due ceremony'. She notified the police of my complaints and wrote to her MP, John Butcher, telling him that I had made a groundless complaint to the university about her presence near my home. I too looked to authority to back up my complaints, and the consequent battle between authority and authority – right against right – was to become a recurring feature of the case.

I later learnt from my neighbours, Malcolm and Sandra Martin, that Mrs M and her husband had been coming to my house at least since July 1994 and had been spending substantial periods of time watching it. Sandra Martin recounted that she first saw Mrs M in the summer of 1994, walking up and down my road and continually gazing at my house, as if she was looking for someone. According to her report, Mrs M then appeared in a dark-coloured car and parked opposite my house. She sat in her car and adjusted her rear mirror to an angle where she could watch my kitchen window and driveway. After some considerable time a visitor arrived and Mrs M drove off, but appeared again almost immediately further up the road. She then started once more to walk up and down the road, gazing at my place. From this time, my neighbour concluded, 'I have become more and more aware of this lady'.

I too became more and more aware of this lady in the autumn of 1994. When teaching started again in October, Mrs M used to wait for me each Thursday morning around ten o'clock outside my seminar room. She would not say anything, just hang about the lobby making her presence felt and watching me. On other occasions she stood for up to an hour in the courtyard of the Social Studies building looking up to my office window. Sometimes she waited outside my lecture rooms for me to walk past. Sometimes she came late in the evening with her husband to our department and examined the noticeboards – especially staff photographs. They also began to spend more time outside my house. Once I returned home around nine o'clock on a dark November night to find Mrs M at the end of my driveway. I wondered at her commitment to standing in the cold and asked her to leave. She walked slowly to where her husband had parked his car, the two of them then drove past my house, turned their car and slowly passed my house again. I took down their registration number and wrote to the university expressing more concern.

During this same autumn of 1994 a series of mysterious incidents occurred involving my car. As I was leaving the university late one evening, I discovered that my car had been broken into, and with what must have been considerable violence the steering wheel had been wrenched off. Two weeks later my car was broken into again and the windows and doors were further damaged. A week after that one of the mirrors was broken at the university. As these acts of vandalism multiplied, I started to suspect Mrs M. It was unusual for a car to be targeted three times in four weeks in the same university car park with no apparent intention to steal it. It may also have been significant that these incidents always occurred on a Thursday – the day that Mrs M used to wait for me outside my seminar room knowing that I taught there for three hours without a break. I had seen her walking towards the multi-storey car park after she left this building. My suspicions were reinforced when the second wing mirror was broken off – this time in my driveway.

Coincidences do occur, however, and I was keen not to jump to conclusions. In search of further evidence I arranged with the university for my car to be watched by a security officer on the following Thursday morning (24 November 1994). True to form, Mrs M was outside my seminar room at ten. She later made her way to the multi-storey car park and looked around until she found my car. Bill Elkin, the security guard, saw Mrs M approach it around eleven and wrote in his report:

> The lady in the picture which I had, arrived at the car park, walking to the car from behind me. She stood in the gangway and looked around with no one else on the floor. She went down the side of the Peugeot to the front and took a good long look at the windscreen and all along the side. She then came to the gangway, stood looking at the car rear, then went down the passenger side and did the same again. On this side she took out her glasses and bent down to read something on the passenger seat area. She replaced her glasses in the case and then walked off . . .

If Bill's account hardened my prejudices, they were galvanised two days later when I woke up to find an empty space in my driveway where my car had been parked. It was stolen. After the theft Robin Cohen, a friend and colleague, drove me to where Mr and Mrs M lived to see if we could spot the car. It took us some time to find her house, since her road was not marked on the Coventry *A to Z*, but eventually we discovered a fairly large, detached house with a double garage and many signs of electronic alarms. The car was nowhere in sight and after looking around the area for a few minutes we gave up our quest. On the way back to the university, we dropped into the local police station to report the unusual circumstances of the theft and to ask the police if they would question Mr and Mrs M about it. The duty officer brimmed with reluctance: there would be no car available to go to her house, my suspicions were not strongly enough based, she would simply decline to answer questions, there are many car thefts, etc.

Next day an officer from Leamington (a different police area from Coventry) told me that a well-known local thief had been seen driving my car so I could discount any suspicion that Mrs M was involved. I asked the police to question the suspect about the background to the theft and whether anyone had put him up to it. I heard nothing for over a month until I received a phone call out of the blue saying that the police had been mistaken about this 'car thief' and had no idea who stole my car. The car itself had been found a week after the theft: its recently repaired wing mirrors, the power-steering and exhaust system had all been damaged. I was frustrated by what I saw as police inaction. My expectation that they would investigate my suspicions proved quite unrealistic.

On the day after my car was found, Mr and Mrs M were outside my house again. They walked up and down peering into my windows for well over half an hour until Mr M went off to fetch his car. He struck me as a brute of a man, shorter and squatter than his wife, but for the first time I noticed how similar their faces were – like cousins. Mrs M stood staring at me through my front window with what I described at the time as a 'fixed smile' on her face. I couldn't help feeling that this woman and her husband were gloating over their successes on the car crime front. I was getting very worried by the course of events.

That evening a bizarre incident occurred. I went out to see a film, came back about eleven and was on the phone to a friend when I realised how cold the house was. I discovered that all the radiators had been turned off at the valves and a hot water tap in the bathroom had been left running. There was no signs of a break-in and the doors were secure, but I could find no explanation other than that someone must have entered the house. I phoned the Leamington police who advised me that, since nothing had been stolen, there was no sign of break-in and no violence had occurred, this was a civil trespass, not a criminal offence, and that they accordingly had no role to play. Again police inaction.

My view was that Mr and Mrs M were doing their worst to frighten me but I wondered whether I was getting paranoid. I called a friend round to talk it over and then placed a large stick close to my bed – just in case of further entries.

Bit by bit the harassment intensified. One Sunday morning I was washing up the dishes from the night before in that dishevelled way that wants the world to vanish, when through unfocused eyes I saw Mrs M standing at an angle to my house and staring into my kitchen window. She seemed determined to make her presence felt. She stood there for a few minutes, walked slowly on to the common, disappeared behind some trees, reappeared some minutes later, and stood looking once more. There was something about her that now sent a shiver down my spine.

The next day I arrived at work to find that someone had got into my office: papers were strewn over the table and the floor, what I described as 'murky liquid' had been poured into the metal wastepaper basket and a roll of toilet paper was curiously unwrapped, re-wrapped and left on my desk. Nothing was actually stolen. What had been left, I thought, was a sign of entry and a signature of the anonymous entrant.

On the following Sunday morning I was still half asleep and doing up my dressing-gown when I opened the lounge curtains to find Mrs M looking straight at me. She walked slowly around my house, many times, then stood staring into my dining room while I ate breakfast. When I waved her away, she gave a little wave back and fixed that same triumphant smile. It was one of those times when the world itself seemed to lose all warmth.

Later that morning I was on the phone to my friend Marion Doyen when I went out to see if Mrs M was still around. Within a minute she drove up in her car, stopped where I was standing, wound down the window of the passenger door and said some words which I could not properly hear. She looked daggers. I took a deep breath and decided to confront her. I told her that what she was doing was *stalking* me: I think that this was the first time that I had publicly given 'it' a name – even to myself. I called her *malicious* and *mad* – the only words I could immediately find to capture that sense of hatred loitering and lurking on my threshold. I told her to seek psychological help and threatened trouble with the university and the law.

Her reply was as scoffing as it was forthright: she had

been round my house many times and had checked with the police that she was fully entitled to do so. Nothing was going to stop her and the university had no jurisdiction over what she did in her spare time. Marion, still on the other end of the phone, overheard some of the exchange and in a note to the university wrote:

Mrs M refused to go and said continually: 'I've got a right to be here' ... at one point I heard her very clearly saying: 'I've walked round here a thousand times and I'll come a thousand times more' ... Robert said that she should get help, that none of this had anything to do with any actions of his, and that she must leave him alone.

What I remember best was Mrs M's chilling declaration that I had *destroyed* her the previous year and now she was going to *destroy* me.

By chance, my former partner drove up with some friends of hers and my daughter. Mrs M drove off and they too drove off without comment. In a state of twofold agitation I threw the phone hopelessly into the hedge. Perhaps I myself was in more need of psychological help than I knew.

Later that day I was calming down with my friend Alan Norrie when Mrs M again walked by my house – this time with her husband. We decided to confront them together. We followed them down the street and up a path until they both turned round and Mrs M started to video us. Her husband was aggressive: he did not like being called 'Angus' and insisted that I deserved what I 'got' because of what I had 'done' to his wife. We pointed out that stalking was not only a nasty, unpleasant thing to do, but potentially illegal. Mrs M dismissed these warnings out of hand: 'I'm *so* scared, I'm *so* scared' was the repeated gist of her scoffing sarcasm. In his description of this encounter for the university Alan wrote:

> Mrs M kept filming and talking, often grinning in an arch, apparently playful way, that seemed quite inappropriate. On the one hand, she says she is simply exercising her citizen's right to use a public pathway, and this happens to bring her past Dr Fine's house on a regular basis; on the other hand, she seems to be pursuing a view that Dr Fine and the university have wronged her and she is trying to build a case against him ... Unfortunately, her husband's language and comments suggested that he endorses his wife's view of events. My impression was that neither was really swayed from an obsessive view of Dr Fine's and the university's conduct in relation to her and that Mrs M will not be deflected from what appears to be what I understand is clinically described as an erotomanic obsession.

Erotomanic obsession! Doubtless Alan was right. The sheer hatred which emanated from Mrs M had the force of an erotic charge. We are all well used to the fusion of love and violence, but in this case I felt that *eros* was so deeply repressed and so successfully transmuted into its opposite as to be scarcely recognisable. Erotomanic or not, one thing was clear: Mrs M would not be deterred.

In the new year of 1995, six months after the stalking began and over a year after Mrs M's first charge, the stalking got progressively worse. One evening I was talking to my neighbour when we saw Mr and Mrs M drive by in her familiar, green Metro. A few minutes later a friend of mine, Jessica Tipping, arrived for dinner and the two of us went out together on the common to take Fudge for a walk. It was dark and Mrs M came after us. Jessica described evocatively what happened:

> Mrs M came very close to us, partially encircled us, walked through the trees behind us and then left. Her approach had a strange combination of intent and denial; she walked straight toward us but having reached us refused any acknowledgement of us ... This was an unnerving and creepy experience. Having heard from Robert about her repeated surveillance of his house, this confirmed in my mind a sense of this woman's invasion of boundaries.

The two of them followed us while we walked on the common and then lingered outside the house. I called the police and to my surprise a squad car came – but it was some twenty minutes later and Mr and Mrs M had left. Again the police said there was nothing they could do.

Another time Sandra Martin rang my bell at about nine in the evening to tell me that Mrs M was standing near my front door. When we went to see what was happening, she walked slowly away behind some trees, was joined by her husband and the two of them then walked back towards us. I said, 'Get lost, Mrs M.' Mrs M said, 'Professional misconduct, Dr Fine, I have a document to prove it.' I said something like: 'Harassment is against the law.' She said (not without some justice): 'You don't even know the law.' Eventually they walked to their car and waited for a few minutes outside my house with their engine running and lights on.

At the university my office was broken into again: my computer was stolen and the same 'signature' was left as before – murky liquid poured into the waste-bin and the toilet roll unfolded and refolded in its distinctive manner. Fortunately there was no hard disk in the computer, so whoever stole it had no access to my files or inner thoughts.

In the spring of 1995 the university began to act on my behalf to discipline Mrs M and I began the process of taking legal action to stop her – I'll say more about both later – but neither had any effect on her actions. During the Easter break I was away for some time, but my neighbours reported that Mr and Mrs M had been frequent visitors to my house. A scent of what was to come could be detected in another incident involving Alan Norrie. Mrs M had been standing opposite my house when Alan and I went outside with a camera to photograph her. This made her irate. She called me a 'bastard' and 'little shit' and Alan my 'little friend'. She seemed to resent the presence of anyone else in the vicinity of her stalking. She said that I was too cowardly to confront her alone. She also said that I had taken away her degree and that all I needed to do was apologise for my conduct.

Her final words puzzled me: 'I would not like to be like you.' Like what? a sociologist, a socialist, an unmarried father, a sexual deviant, an undeserving academic, a Jew? I do not know what image of indecency or impropriety lay behind them. Less cryptically she told me, 'You can stick it up your arse.' Alan described her demeanour as 'venomous' and I concurred.

On most mornings I would take a swim at the leisure centre down the road. It was a precious time for me. I enjoyed this pre-breakfast refreshment of body and soul. I had been introduced to it by Gillian Rose, a friend and colleague who has now died prematurely of cancer. It was she who in her severe style likened the swim to a morning prayer and the great window of the pool to a church altar. I did not quite share these sentiments but took her meaning. She sought to improve my ungainly stroke as she herself battled against untimely and unjust disease.

In April 1995 Mrs M began to follow me down the road to the swimming pool, or wait for me outside the pool and follow me back to my house. One morning I left the pool to find her standing by Fudge, my dog. She seemed startled by my arrival. It looked as though she had given the dog something to eat and the dog vomited for the rest of the day. I don't know if I was being paranoid in seeing a connection. Another morning I was near the pool when I felt someone behind me. I looked round to find Mrs M on my heels. She said that the reports of her actions which I sent the university contravened the Data Protection Act (and indeed soon after her lawyer sent the university a letter to this effect). When I told her once more to stop stalking me, she stuck her tongue out and asked, 'Does it turn you on?' I replied, 'Like a cockroach.' An argument ensued in which she insisted that she would afflict me for ever and a day. A number of fellow-swimmers and one of the staff came on the scene to find out what was wrong. I said that Mrs M was stalking me. She countered: 'Play-acting again, Dr Fine.' When I threatened to call the police, she left.

By now Mrs M would come to my house almost every day for weeks on end – followed by some short but vainly hopeful intermissions. She also escalated her activities at the university. What I found most disturbing was when she started to place herself outside the windows of my teaching rooms and gaze in while I was teaching. She began to follow me, one car behind the other, either in town or from my home to work. Sometimes my encounters with her seemed coincidental. Once, for example, we bumped into each other by accident outside a video shop near the police station, but then she stood by my car when I went into the shop. Another evening she and her husband were in the Arts Centre at the university when I arrived for a drink with a friend; they watched us until we left. By this time I was actively planning with my lawyer to take out an injunction.

In the same month, on 24 May 1995, my car was stolen once more – this time from the multi-storey car park at the university. My then partner, Pat Volk, drove me around Mrs M's house to look for my car but to no avail. As soon as we approached her house, however, her face appeared at the window. Again the police failed to question either Mr or Mrs M and I never saw the car again. I received a letter from Mrs M's solicitor, saying that I had made 'various unfounded allegations' against his client to the effect that she was in some way involved in the damage and thefts. He said that these allegations were emphatically denied and potentially libellous, and warned me that I would face legal action if I repeated them.

The theft of my car was followed by an intense series of visits outside my house by Mrs M. At the time, I noted: 'I know that what I am about to write is impressionistic, but it was difficult to avoid seeing a triumphant look in her eye.' A flavour of what was happening outside my house may be gained from a note Pat Volk sent to the university a few days later. She wrote:

In the early part of the evening we were in his sitting room which has windows looking out onto Newbold Common. Robert was sitting down working at a table by the window and I was sitting away from the window. At about 8 p.m. he drew my attention to a woman peering over the garden hedge into the room. He told me that this was a Mrs M, a woman whose behaviour had been causing him considerable annoyance and distress for some time. As I sat there, I saw Mrs M walk backwards and forwards in front of the house, then cross over the road where she appeared to be speaking to someone on a mobile phone. I was made to feel extremely uneasy by her behaviour and went across to the window. When she saw me standing there, she began to pace backwards and forwards along the grass. She then waved at me and made an obscene gesture which I experienced as threatening. Mrs M then walked away into the bushes on the Comyn. Shortly afterwards ... I saw her walking past the window again, this time with a man whom I understand to be her husband. Nothing actually happened but the combination of Mrs M's very unusual behaviour and the threatening gesture she made towards me made me feel very uneasy about their appearance outside the house.

Three weeks later Pat had another unfortunate encounter when she and I were taking my dog for a walk on the common. Mr and Mrs M followed us. As we turned back, they came towards us and Mrs M called Pat a 'tart' and a 'bit'. Pat warned her that she was going to call the police – which she did.

In June a new development occurred: Mrs M took to entering the swimming pool while I was there. On the first occasion it made me feel physically sick, but as I grimly discovered, one can get used to anything. A pattern emerged: she followed me from my home or waited at the pool; she then came into the water with me, swam near me for a while and watched me swim from the Jacuzzi; she got out when I got out and thanks to quick changing was waiting for me outside the pool by the time I left; she would then hide behind a little copse opposite the leisure centre, emerge from the shadows of the trees as I passed and follow me closely as I walked home. Once near my home, she would quickly overtake me and double back, coming close to my face and muttering insults. Then she would walk up and down either directly outside my house or on the common while I took breakfast, and sometimes disappear into the woods at the rear of the common only to reappear some minutes later. Often I could see her shadowy outline camouflaged in the woods. This pattern of behaviour lasted many months. Occasionally she would be accompanied by one of her daughters or her husband.

Each time I saw her, a wave of anxiety would flow over me. My breathing would become difficult to control and I felt indignation, disgust and a sense of utter invasion course through my body. Then I would push these to the back of my mind until the next encounter.

I tried not to be passive in the face of this vendetta. I asked the management of the leisure centre to bar Mrs M from the pool, at least while I was there in the mornings, on the grounds that she was using it to stalk one of their customers. The initial response of the deputy manageress was positive, but once she took advice from the head of leisure services and my local community policewoman she became less sure. As far as I can tell, the police-woman said it was beyond her powers to ban Mrs M. My request was finally lost when the manageress came back from holiday. She had no end of reasons for inaction, which went something like this:

1. We have no legal right to bar a member of the public from a public facility.
2. Mrs M has done nothing wrong in the pool.
3. We do not have the resources to police Mrs M's admission to the pool.
4. My private life is no affair of theirs.

I tried to persuade her that the local authority did have the right to bar someone from the use of the pool, that Mrs M was doing something wrong – namely stalking and harassing one of its customers; that the staff at the pool would have no trouble in refusing Mrs M a ticket to enter; and that while it is true to say that my private life is not their problem, the use of their facilities to stalk a customer is their business and might affect their business. My arguments cut no ice.

To muddy the waters further, Mrs M made her own complaint to the management of the leisure centre that I was inciting people in the pool to stare at her and that I had assaulted her. Some of my fellow-swimmers would look at Mr and Mrs M, for they knew what was happening, but in fact most people avoided eye contact. One swimmer who has become a good friend, Nicola Wall, often used to tell me of her sightings of Mrs M (and sometimes her daughter and husband as well) outside my house or the pool. She got nervous on her own behalf when she saw Mrs M carefully examining her car in the leisure centre car park. Regarding the 'assault', what happened was that in front of a fellow-swimmer I called Mr M a 'stalker' when he followed me into the shower, and I said the same to Mrs M when she waited for me outside the men's changing rooms. I wrote at the time:

> Mrs M flared up in a temper, and while I was walking away with my back turned to her, she banged quite forcibly into my back. She then rushed past and started to complain about me to the receptionist at the Centre. Her behaviour was, as usual, thoroughly aggressive.

My fellow-swimmer told me that he later saw Mrs M photograph him as he got into his car and described her behaviour as 'threatening'.

I tried to involve the police. Since September 1994 I had called them many times but it was a frustrating enterprise. They did not pursue my suspicions about the damage to my car, the thefts or the break-ins to my office, pleading lack of resources as well as insufficient evidence, and they consistently maintained that stalking was outside their province. The lack of apparent co-ordination between the Warwickshire and Coventry police forces did not help. The local community WPC was sympathetic until we touched upon the topic of protests at Coventry airport against the export of live animals, but my cups of tea proved of little avail beyond her arranging for a senior officer to interview me in my house. He suggested that if *I* were given an official warning not to 'disturb the peace', this might give the police the chance to arrest Mrs M for behaviour likely to cause a disturbance of the peace. I could just about see his logic but I wasn't much impressed with a suggestion that the stalked should be warned rather than the stalker. It seemed like an Alice in Wonderland proposition, all topsy-turvy, but before I could object I found myself being handed an official warning. Anyway nothing came of it.

One difficulty I faced was that each time I called the police, a different officer was on duty and I had to start from scratch. There seemed to be no co-ordination and no collection of information. Certainly there was no unit organised to deal with cases of harassment and stalking and the lack of criminal law in this area was interpreted as ruling out police action. To be fair, the police came to my house a few times – usually too late to catch Mrs M in the act but once they asked her and her husband a few questions. As far as I can gather, Mr and Mrs M told them that they were enjoying the 'amenities'. One conscientious police constable, PC Ron Pugh, made determined but abortive efforts to construct a case. Once he devised a plan of action to catch Mrs M in the act. One morning I phoned him as I left the pool. As Mrs M followed me, PC Pugh passed us in his police car. I nodded that it was Mrs M behind me. As soon as she saw the police car, however, she simply walked away. Another time he spent over three hours taking a statement from Pat Volk and another three hours taking mine, but nothing was done with the report by superior officers.

There was little or nothing that the police either could or would do except advise me to take out a civil injunction. My frustration reminded me of reports I had read of women who were victims of domestic violence, who complained that their perceptions were not validated or taken seriously by the police. I was used to my words being given some credibility, so it was a 'learning experience' not to be listened to.

By this time Mr and Mrs M were regularly haunting my local pub. I think their routine was this: they ordered drinks, Mrs M went off for half an hour's stalking, when she came back they drank up and went off to do a bit of stalking together, and then he would go off to get their car. Their presence certainly put me off having a casual drink – particularly if I was alone. Once when I went in with some friends Mr and Mrs M were sitting at the corner table. Mrs M got up and stood next to me with that demonic grin on her face while I ordered drinks at the bar. Then she walked up and down by our table. I asked the pub manager whether she and her husband could be barred. He said that he did not have enough evidence to go on – only my word.

One date sticks in my mind. On 13 July 1995 my legal initiatives bore fruit. Mrs M gave an undertaking to a judge in the High Court not to harass or molest me, not to interfere with my property and not to walk on the pavement outside my house. Next morning, however, she was waiting outside my house from seven o'clock, followed me into the swimming pool, waited for me outside, followed me back again to my house, and then walked around outside my house for three-quarters of an hour. Business as usual.

During the summer holiday of 1995 I went climbing in the French Alps. I experienced the tricks that being stalked can play on the mind when I imagined I saw Mrs M on a mountain path and dreamed that I saw her falling down a crevasse. The unconscious does not take vacations. When I returned home, my neighbour told me that she and her family had seen Mrs M photographing their house. They called the police, who said that no offence had been committed and that they could not intervene. Later that night my neighbours' garage was burgled and several thousand pounds' worth of fishing equipment stolen. The police declined to treat Mr and Mrs M as suspects – or to question them.

In October another of my neighbours told me that he had again seen the woman who had 'repeatedly lurked and watched your house earlier this summer' outside my house. He wrote:

I was startled to hear a strange woman's voice say 'I'll have you know that the Vice-Chancellor has ruled that I can take my case to court, so you can stop staring at me'. I replied that ... she was being a silly girl and making a nuisance of herself ... She replied with 'I am not a silly girl, I'm a woman!' This retort was followed by 'Why are you watching me? I have a perfect right to be here'. I replied with 'I can watch whoever I wish to watch, it's a free country', to which she replied 'exactly'.

(This neighbour did admit that his wife had left him on the grounds of incurable condescension.)

Another date to remember: my fiftieth birthday, 16 November 1995. I found Mrs M as usual waiting for me outside the swimming pool at about 8 a.m. Again she followed me into the pool and then back again to my house after my swim. I had the sense of having been given an indefinite sentence. I cried in a quiet corner of the pool. Nicola Wall comforted me. 'Just ignore her,' was her advice. It was difficult to follow.

An incident to remember: I was trying to lecture to forty students and felt the cold, persistent stare of Mrs M as she looked in through the window of the lecture hall. For once I found it impossible to block out her invasive presence and get on with the lecture. After half an hour or so, I asked my class to take a break and went upstairs to phone Cathy Charlton, the deputy registrar's assistant. In intemperate langauge, I asked her to call the security officers: 'Get that fucking woman away from me' is what I said. She did with customary efficiency but after the lecture Mrs M followed me into the Social Studies courtyard. A few of my colleagues happened to pass and I was gratified when they gave her a mouthful of advice. There was a verbal altercation until the head of security, Royce Farr, arrived. He took Mrs M aside and talked with her at some length. From their body language I guessed (rightly) that they knew each other. She had after all worked for the police and he was an ex-superintendent. Later Royce came up to my office where he enjoined me to apologise to Cathy for swearing in front of her (which I did), send her flowers (which I did not) and warned me that I was undermining his plan of action: 'softly, softly, catchee monkey'. Rightly or not, I was beginning to feel, as so often is reported, that it is the

victim who gets the blame. I would have preferred it if
he had told me that he knew Mrs M.

These were disheartening times. It was over two years
since the beginning of this 'affair'. The sky was grey, the
days were short, and the stalking was worse than ever. I
had lost my car. I had lost the pleasure of my morning
swims. I had lost in my attempt to have my stalker
banned from the swimming pool or the pub. I had lost in
my efforts at involving the police. Loss was in the air.
Disciplinary action at the university and legal action in
the courts had produced no results on the ground. My
friends' words of advice on how to deal with her face to
face – ignore her, confront her, throw water upon her,
invite her in for a cup of tea, hire a private detective, call
up a hit squad, entrap her or worse – were well meant
but somehow beside the point. There seemed to be
nowhere to turn. The stalker was becoming my shadow.

It is difficult to capture the grindingly repetitive
character of being the target of such an obsession. Mrs M
was almost daily outside my house. Sometimes she
followed me in her car around town and I would have to
shake her off. Sometimes she followed me to work.
Sometimes she followed my friends when they left the
house. Sometimes she photographed me and my friends
as we were going in or out of the house. Sometimes she
photographed my neighbours and their house. Sometimes she took notes as she watched. Sometimes she
kerb-crawled me. Sometimes she shouted abuse or
threatened me. There wasn't much left that was private.
Uncertainty about when she would return, how long the
stalking would continue, whether she was responsible
for the thefts and vandalism, what escalation might occur
made me anxious.

During this period I was keeping a diary which I regularly sent to the university for safe-keeping. I was not completely consistent, for there were times when the sheer repetitiveness of the phenomenon made it seem pointless, when I despaired of finding any resolution to this saga, when I simply wanted to push the business as far as possible from my mind and get on with the rest of my life. Nonetheless it was a compelling discipline to write about these events with the pressures posed by an external agency in mind. I am sure that if the diary had just been for myself, I would have been even less consistent.

Beneath the formality of my reports to the university, I had difficulty in expressing the sense of invasion which Mrs M's persistent, impertinent presence forced upon me, or the anxiety that would run through my body when she approached me, or the rage I would suppress for fear of lashing out at her (or her husband), or the dismay that my work and my friendships might be suffering. I experienced stalking as an indefinite sentence: if there were an injunction, she would ignore it; if she went to gaol, she would soon come out; if she fell under a bus, her husband or daughter would carry on the family tradition.

Diary Extracts, 1996

Thursday 4 January
I saw Mrs M outside my house between 10 and 10.45 a.m. She simply stood on the common opposite looking at me through the windows of my house. Then she followed me when I took my dog for a walk. She was outside the house when I left by car and was still there when I returned five minutes later. I took some photos of her, though she turned her back to the camera.

Monday 8 January
Mrs M was loitering outside my house between about 9.15 a.m. and 9.30 a.m. when I left by car for the university.

Wednesday 10 January
I saw Mrs M standing in the courtyard of the Social Studies building looking up to my room for 5 to 10 minutes around 11 a.m.

Thursday 11 January
I returned home at about 8 p.m. I saw Mrs M waiting outside my house on the common opposite. I took my dog for a walk and Mrs M, now joined by her husband, followed me for its duration (about 10 minutes). While they were following me, Mrs M called me many names – 'you stupid little creep' sticks in mind. She told me several times that she would win, she had every right to be on the common and that I did not even know the law. Then she began to threaten me, saying that this is only

the start and that there was worse to come. Later that evening I went to the Newbold Comyn Arms with two student friends. Mr and Mrs M were drinking in the corner of the pub. Apart from Mrs M wandering around our table and standing by me at the bar, not much else happened.

Tuesday 16 January

I was teaching my Social Theory of Law course in the law seminar room when I noticed Mrs M looking up at the window of the room from the lawn opposite. She wandered around there for at least 45 minutes and I informed Cathy of what was happening.

Wednesday 24 January

As I was leaving my home at around 9.15 a.m. I saw Mrs M walking up and down outside my house. One of my fellow-swimmers reports that she stopped outside earlier in her car. At the university I saw her in the Social Studies enclosure walking around and looking up to my office window. When I went to teach in So.10 at 12 noon, she was outside waiting for me to arrive. While I was teaching, she spent the whole hour opposite my window looking in and sometimes gesticulating. When a security guard passed her, she turned her back and hid her face. As I came out of the lecture room, she was waiting outside the door. She followed me as I was talking to students. Then I had to dash to Car Park 7 to drive to a meeting, but she beat me to it and was already waiting outside the car park.

Thursday 25 January

As I was coming into the Social Studies building shortly before 10 a.m. I heard footsteps running behind and then closely past me. Yes, it was Mrs M. I told her to go away. She ran to the

Physics building, went in and out a few times and then ran off towards the Athletics building.

Thursday 1 February
Mrs M hovered for about half an hour between about 11 and 11.30 a.m. in the Social Studies courtyard looking into my window while I was speaking with one of my students.

Saturday 3 February
Mrs M was outside my house between 8.30 a.m. and 9 a.m. walking up and down and passing on the pavement directly next to my property.

Sunday 4 February
Mrs M outside my house in early afternoon seen by myself, my former partner and my daughter.

Thursday 8 February
Mrs M was seen by a friend of mine taking photos of my house around 9.30 a.m.

Saturday 10 February
Mrs M seen by myself and a friend, Steve Alleyne, walking up and down outside my house looking into my windows for about half an hour from 9.30 to 10 a.m. She walked on the pavement right next to my property several times.

Sunday 11 February
Mr and Mrs M were seen by myself, Charles Turner (from Sociology) and Dave Hirsh (a Sociology graduate student) outside my house for about an hour between 12.30 and 1.30 p.m.

Wednesday 14 February
Mrs M was outside my house – including on the pavement directly outside – on two occasions: early and late afternoon.

Friday 16 February
Mrs M was walking up and down on pavement directly outside my house from 9.30 to 10.15 a.m.

Sunday 18 February
Mrs M was outside my house, walking on pavement directly next to my property, from about 3 p.m. to 4 p.m.

Friday 23 February
At 8.30 a.m. Mrs M was waiting for me outside the swimming pool. She was still there when I left at 9.15 a.m. The receptionist at the swimming pool told me that Mrs M had spoken to the manageress of the pool, saying that she was going to start swimming again and did not want anyone to look at her strangely.

Saturday 24 February
At about 5 p.m. Mr and Mrs M walked up and down outside my house for at least 45 minutes, staring into the windows and passing within inches of my front hedge. When I left to go to London, Mr M was on his mobile phone and Mrs M made some rather rude gesture toward me. I was concerned about the security of my empty house . . .

Tuesday 27 February
Around 9 a.m. Mrs M was outside my house for at least 40 minutes looking in through the windows. She then followed me to the university – her car directly behind my own. I stopped my car en route to inform her that I objected to being followed in my car and to request her to stop. This was witnessed by

another driver and then Mrs M did slow down and let him overtake her.

Wednesday 28 February
Between 11 a.m. and 12 noon Mrs M was in the courtyard of the Social Studies building looking straight up into the window of my room. She was also seen by the student who was in the room, Zoe W, and by various members of staff in Sociology. She followed me over to my lecture room (So.10) and then placed herself right outside the window of the room staring straight at me while I lectured. When I left the room I was again followed by Mrs M. A number of my colleagues arrived, who recognised her and also added their three pennies' worth about the undesirability of her behaviour. While I was working in my office in the evening, I noticed both Mr and Mrs M waiting in the Social Studies courtyard looking into the window of my room for over 30 minutes. When I left for the car park, Mr and Mrs M walked directly in front of me and waited outside the car park for my car to leave.

Friday 1 March
Mrs M followed me from the swimming pool to my house at about 9.30 a.m. She walked up and down (including on the pavement outside my house) staring into the windows. I took a photo of her. Sometimes she lurked in the woods opposite my home. When I walked to work at about 11 a.m. to catch the bus, she stopped her car right by me and called out something unintelligible. I took another photo of her.

Tuesday 5 March
Mrs M was waiting for me outside the swimming pool at about 9.15 a.m. She followed me to my house and made a point of coming up very close to me. I told her once again to stop

stalking me. She was still outside the house when I left for work.

Wednesday 6 March
Mrs M was in the swimming pool when I arrived at about 8 a.m. She stayed in or around the pool until I left. When I left the pool, she was already outside my house (a quick changer). Since she was only a few feet from my hedge, I told her that she was violating her undertaking to the court not to come within 30 feet of my property. She denied that she had any such undertaking. I tape-recorded our conversation which lasted about 5 minutes.

Sunday 10 March
Mrs M is waiting outside my house in the dark, wearing black, at about 9 to 9.30 p.m.

Wednesday 13 March
Mrs M is outside my house when I leave for the university with Steve Alleyne, at about 9.20 a.m. When I am lecturing in So.10 I see Mrs M outside the window.

Friday 15 March
Mrs M walks up and down outside my house peering into the windows around 9.15 a.m. and is there until I leave for work.

Sunday 17 March
I think it was about 9.30 a.m. when I see Mr and Mrs M walk up and down outside my house. I do not know how long they stayed. I am beginning to realise that I am now constantly apprehensive of when and where she might turn up. Her intrusiveness is without bounds.

Monday 18 March

I see Mrs M going past me in her car while I take my dog for a walk at around 7.30 a.m. She turns her car round at the end of the road and parks it near the swimming pool. She goes in just ahead of me and then waits at the entrance of the women's changing room to make herself observed. I tell her sarcastically that I know that she is there and that the doctor will be coming soon. She waits for me outside the changing rooms and then walks just ahead of me into the pool. She stays in the pool while I swim. While walking back home, I see her hovering outside my house. She must be a rapid changer. She makes a point of walking right up to me as I return home. Then she hovers around the house until I leave for work. What does one do with someone as mad and offensive as she is?

Tuesday 19 March

At about 8 a.m. Mrs M follows me into the swimming pool. She stays in the pool as long as I swim. When I walk back home, she is already waiting outside and makes a point of walking right up to me.

Wednesday 20 March

Mrs M is seen by some of my fellow-swimmers outside my house at about 9.15 a.m. I have already taken my daughter to school and went straight to work. When I return to the house at about 8.45 p.m., I sit in the car in the driveway for a few minutes listening to the end of a radio programme about the memoirs of an Albanian refugee. When I step out of the car, I see Mrs M in the dark at the end of the driveway.

Thursday 21 March

About 8 a.m. I go to the swimming pool. About 8.15 a.m. Mrs M follows me in. She stays in the pool until I leave. Walking back to my house (about 9.15 a.m.), I see Mrs M already hovering on the common opposite. She makes a point of crossing the road and walking right up to me as I approach the house. I ask her if she has ever spent time in a mental hospital. She seemed perturbed by the question. I see her car leave shortly after. Then minutes later, she is again walking up and down outside my house looking into my windows and continues until at least 10.30 a.m. I saw her running away from the front hedge at about this time. At about 5.45 p.m. Mrs M walks up and down outside my house with her husband. I tell them both to go away and he calls me a 'shit' and she calls me 'a little man'. I cannot describe how intrusive and disgusting they are.

Friday 22 March
This morning Mrs M has anticipated me in the swimming pool. She swims a little and watches me a lot in the pool. It is creepy but it seems that one can get used to anything. Her car is still in the car park when I leave, and she as ever is already outside my house. She stays outside until at least about 9.45 a.m.

Saturday 23 March
Mr and Mrs M are outside my house from about 4–6 p.m. When I go on to the common with my daughter and a friend of hers, Mrs M shouts some rude comments at me – calling me an (inaudible) 'little man'. They are seen by a friend, Steve Alleyne, for most of this period and at one point Mrs M walked up to my neighbour, Malcolm, while he was walking his dog.

Sunday 24 March
My colleague Charles Turner, who now lives up the street,

reports that Mrs M observed him leaving his flat. I was not at home.

Monday 25 March
Mrs M follows me into the swimming pool at about 8 a.m. and then walks up and down outside my house after the swim until 10 a.m. She is seen by my friends Charles Turner and Nicola Wall.

Tuesday 26 March
I am in London but Steve Alleyne reports to me that Mrs M was outside my house for at least an hour between about 6.30 and 7.30 p.m. When he walked my dog, she followed him. He was not pleased.

Wednesday 27 March
Mrs M is outside my house as I take my daughter to her piano lesson at 6.45 p.m.

Thursday 28 March
Mrs M follows me into the swimming pool and then kerb-crawls in her car by me as I am walking back from the pool. Each time one has to shrug it off.

Friday 29 March
As I leave for work at about 8.15 a.m. I see Mrs M coming towards my house in her car. She is looking daggers. Mrs M seems to be getting worse. She is entirely impenetrable to argument and her husband, less intelligent than her and seeming quite inarticulate except for the occasional swear word, is no better. They seem to have a mission to destroy and I am the target. Generally, I stay reasonably cool and detached and do not think much about her when I am at work. But constant pressure like this takes its toll. I find myself looking

around more than I should and spend quite a lot of time thinking about this mad creature. A number of my friends have commented on their own fears in relation to her. I am too used to her presence to be afraid, but the whole matter has become extremely burdensome. She needs psychiatric treatment. If she does not get it, who knows where it will end. Let us hope that the forthcoming legal suit will set things in motion.

Wednesday 28 August

It is a long time since I have written to you regarding Mrs M and her antics. This is not because she has in any way desisted from her activities, but rather because I simply ran out of steam in recording them. She has in fact been stalking me persistently, sometimes with her husband, sometimes with her daughter, but usually alone. She has been outside my house, staring into the windows, walking up and down, observing me from the common opposite for up to two hours a day; she has been following me to the swimming pool, coming into the swimming pool while I am there, waiting for me in the bushes after swimming, following me to my home, and approaching very close to me both at the pool and outside my house. This has been going on regularly – quite often up to five or six days a week. As time goes on, I find her presence increasingly invasive, disturbing and threatening. So much so that I could not bear thinking or writing about it when she was not actually present. Thus the absence of reports from me. My friends – Jeff Rudin, Steve Alleyne and Dave Hirsh – have seen her countless times. Steve and Dave could testify to this effect. Jeff has returned now to South Africa but has left a letter testifying to his observations.

In the recent past I can record the following incidents in more detail.

Sunday 18 August

In the afternoon, Mrs M and her husband walk up and down outside my house for over an hour. Mrs M spends about 20 minutes on the pavement directly next to my hedges staring into my living room, often on tiptoe.

Tuesday 20 August

Mrs M follows me to the swimming pool, waits for me outside the trees, follows me to my home, and then stares in through the windows for about an hour.

Wednesday 21 August

Mrs M is outside my house for about one and a half hours in the morning.

Thursday 22 August

Mrs M steals up behind me as I am approaching the swimming pool at about 8.15 a.m. She follows me into the pool, she waits for me outside the pool (in the trees opposite) as I leave at about 9.15 a.m., she follows me to my house, and then she lingers outside for over an hour. At one point, I came out of my house and shouted at her to get away. She called me a liar, a little creep and other epithets, and reaffirmed that in her view she had every right to do what she is doing.

Sunday 25 August

Mr and Mrs M are outside my house in the morning for about an hour.

Tuesday 27 August

Mrs M and her daughter appear in the swimming pool about 8.30 a.m. and stand right next to where I am swimming.

These are only the last week's events but this week is not abnormal. She is clearly determined to harass me beyond human endurance, and she is in clear contravention of the undertakings which she has given to the court not to harass or molest me and not to walk on the pavement immediately outside my home. Many people in the swimming pool could testify to her activities. Perhaps Nicola Wall could testify on behalf of all of them, but I could ask some of the others as well.

Tuesday 1 October
Around 9 a.m. Mrs M walks up and down outside my house and stares into the window of the kitchen while I am there. Around 8 p.m. Mr and Mrs M are outside my house while I am entertaining Prof. Peter Wagner and his wife Heidrun Friese. When we go out in the car, they [the Ms] make a point of being observed.

Thursday 3 October
Around 8.30 a.m. Mrs M outside my house.

Friday 4 October
Around 8.30 a.m. Mrs M outside my home. Witnessed by a friend who arrived, Dr Gillian Bendelow.

Saturday 5 October
Around 9.30 a.m. Mrs M outside my house, staring in, for at least half an hour.

Tuesday 8 October
9 a.m. As I leave my house, I see Mrs M opposite my house. I drive off ignoring her.

 8.00 p.m. Mrs M is outside my house.

68

Wednesday 9 October

9.00 a.m. By chance, I pass Mrs M walking down Gibbet Hill Road to the university. Cannot get away from her! Lunchtime: Mrs M waiting outside the Arts Centre while I lunch with Peter Wagner. She is seen by him. Around 8 p.m. Mr and Mrs M park down the road. When Steve Alleyne and his partner leave my house in their car, the Ms follow them in theirs to the Spa Centre. Steve is most upset by this.

Thursday 10 October

7.45 a.m. As I open the curtains, I see Mrs M staring in. I drive off ten minutes later with her shouting something from the side of the road.

Friday 11 October

Around 10 a.m. I see Mrs M staring into the kitchen window, then hovering outside my house. I think she has gone away, but as I drive off to the university, she follows me in her car to the university. I take some photos of this incident.

PS: I am not going swimming at present, on account of very painful arms and legs. Thus the absence of swimming pool incidents.

Saturday 12 October

From about 8.30 a.m. Mr and Mrs M are outside my house for over an hour. They take photos of a guest arriving, Dr Gillian Bendelow, and our leaving the house in a car around 10 a.m.

Monday 14 October

Around 9.15 a.m. Mrs M takes photos of me as I leave for work.

Tuesday 15 *October*
Mrs M stands opposite the house and walks on the pavement immediately outside looking in through the windows. She watches me leave the house (standing as ever right by where my car goes) at about 9 a.m.

Thursday 17 October
Mrs M walks up and down outside my home from at least 8.30 a.m. I see her walk down the road around 9.30. She sits in her car watching my house in her mirror, as far as I could tell. I leave for the university at 10 a.m. and go the other way to avoid her following me. Steve Alleyne arrives as I leave. He sees Mrs M turn her car round and try to follow me. She did not catch me up – thankfully.

Friday 18 October
I am sitting in my room in the brand new Social Studies building (P7–2.37) talking to an MA student when I see Mrs M pass my open door and looking in. It was about 3.30 p.m. (I think) . . .

Sunday 20 October
About 6.30 p.m. I go for a walk with a friend, Jessica Tipping, and my dog. When we get outside, we see Mr and Mrs M waiting immediately opposite my house on the Comyn. We walk towards the golf course and lose sight of them as it was getting quite dark. It was a fairly long walk and we return about three-quarters of an hour later. As we pass the swimming pool, rather deep in conversation, Mrs M suddenly emerges from behind a bush clapping her hands furiously above her head and shouting something which I think was that she had recorded our conversation. She continued to clap her hands in the middle of the road for some time. Ms Tipping (who was very perturbed by the shock of the incident) and

myself continued our walk past my house to the end of Newbold Terrace East. I saw Mrs M's car go by. As we were walking back towards my house, Mrs M was following us almost directly opposite on the Comyn. It was quite dark by now. She followed us to the house. When we got in, I asked Steve Alleyne and another friend, Dave, to come out and witness Mrs M while I took a photo of her. When we came out, Mrs M ran into the bushes. We followed her near the bushes and heard this movement through the undergrowth. Suddenly she rushed out and held me by my shirt and did a kind of mock posing for the photos I was trying to take. Unfortunately, my camera does not take photos easily in the dark (it's too automatic) and it did not work. Mrs M then started pointing to her husband (who was hiding behind some trees) and shouting that she was being assaulted by three men. She seemed to be saying that he was filming the incident, but I am not sure. At this point, we returned inside the house. I thought it might be wise to ask Jessica Tipping, Steve Alleyne and David K to write down their accounts, which they each did shortly afterwards. I enclose them with this note.

Monday 21 October
I cannot describe how annoying this woman is. I should add that I did go for some sessions with a psychotherapist partly in order to talk this unpleasant experience through. It was reasonably helpful but over for the present. Mrs M is manifestly getting worse. She is severely interrupting the enjoyment of my home and property; she is deeply disturbing many of my friends and colleagues; she poses a threatening presence for my daughter; and she is constantly and directly violating the terms of her undertaking to the court. She is also extremely time-consuming (I have not determined a rate per

hour yet!) I cannot tolerate her inside the Sociology Department.

Sunday 27 October
Steve Alleyne sees Mr and Mrs M driving past my house very slowly in the evening (about 8 p.m. I think).

Monday 28 October
I see Mrs M outside my house from about 8 a.m. I then see her enter her car, which was parked just down the road, and wait in it watching for me to leave. I finally leave about 9.15 with my daughter and a friend of hers. Mrs M begins to follow us but I lose her at traffic lights.

Tuesday 29 October
Mr and Mrs M drive past my house several times around 8 p.m. While Steve Alleyne, Dr Bendelow and my daughter were in my driveway, fixing the lights of a car, the Ms stop their car at the end of my driveway and Mrs M laughs loudly and in a rather creepy manner. My daughter tells me that she wishes to accompany me while I go out, since she does not want to be in the house with 'that woman' outside.

Thursday 31 October
Around 10.30 a.m. Mrs M is in the Sociology corridor. She asks our secretary, Betty Horner, various questions but without response. I then see her pass my door a couple of times.

3
The University

From the start I had kept in close touch with university officers about the stalking. The reports I wrote to the university were to prove extremely valuable in future proceedings. The act of sending reports served as a discipline on writing and the act of writing put me in a more reflective position and gave me some sense of control. The reports not only functioned as an *aide-mémoire* but through their concurrence with events and detail possessed a definite legitimacy and claim to truth.

As early as autumn 1994 I asked the university to take action against Mrs M in accord with its own statutes. I believed that the university had an obligation not to allow the systematic harassment and intimidation of one member of the university by another. I saw this obligation as deriving in part from the university's own disciplinary code, in part from the type of academic community it seeks to be, and in part from the general responsibility which belongs to all social institutions not to be indifferent to oppression. To be sure, the university is a seat of power which should be used sparingly, but I thought that abuse of power can derive from inaction as well as from excess of action. In any case I needed the support of this institution for which I had worked for many years and which had after all exposed me to the dangers, difficulties and distress associated with teaching this woman.

At first, the university's solicitors advised it that Mrs M's conduct did not fall under the jurisdiction of its regulations and that any interference would only inflame the situation. Their view at this time was that the harassment was a private matter between myself and Mrs M, and that it was up to me to contact the police or my solicitor if I wanted action. I rejected this advice and repeatedly nagged the university to initiate disciplinary proceedings: 'I could not imagine a clearer case of harassment,' I wrote. I was convinced that the longer Mrs M was allowed to get away with harassment without penalty, the more difficult it would be to stop her.

To make my case, I had to substantiate several points of argument. First, I had to demonstrate that Mrs M was in fact engaged in a purposeful form of harassment – an attempt to punish me for my alleged earlier sins – and that I was not a hapless, paranoid victim of accidental encounters, as she claimed. Second, I had to show that the university had the right to intervene in what happens off-campus and to counter the argument that what is done away from the campus is outside its jurisdiction. I argued that the social space which an institution occupies is not so geographically bound. Imagine, I wrote to the university, that

arising out of an academic relationship, a student physically attacked or sought to bribe a lecturer outside University grounds. Would not such behaviour constitute a violation of University rules? I find it hard to believe that all actions committed between members of the University which occur outside University property are *ultra vires* as far as the applicability of University rules is concerned. Whether an act

74

occurs within the University's geographical bounds is surely not the primary issue. The main question must be whether or not the act offends against the norms of proper academic conduct.

Later, when I read Professor Zellick's official *Report on Student Disciplinary Proceedings* (1994), I discovered that in his view too a disciplinary offence need not occur physically on university property; what is crucial is the involvement of its members. Public space is an arena of power and responsibility that is socially rather than physically bounded. Third, I had to distinguish between the evidence needed to take civil or criminal action and that required for the university to enforce its own rules and regulations. I was unaware at the time of Professor Zellick's advice to universities to proceed with extreme caution where a student's alleged misconduct would also constitute a serious *criminal* offence (like the theft of a car), and not to replicate the criminal law in miniature with a lesser quality of evidence. However, stalking was not then a criminal offence. Finally, I needed to show that this was not merely a private dispute and that the university had a responsibility to fulfil.

I was frustrated by the legal advice which the university was receiving, but my efforts were not in vain. The university set up a video security device in my home and office in case there was any escalation of harassment – a common feature in 'stalker' behaviour – and in February 1995 it finally decided to take internal disciplinary action. This promise of institutional support felt like a big breakthrough. In March 1995 a Discipline Committee was convened – consisting of three senior academics, two representatives of the students' union and a legal counsel

– to consider a charge of harassment brought against Mrs
M. The charge read as follows:

> The behaviour in question consists of a number of
> separate incidents which collectively amount to har-
> assment causing Dr Fine concern and distress and
> seriously infringing the proper relationship between a
> member of the academic staff ... and a student. You
> have variously driven past, walked past, loitered
> outside, occupied a parked car outside and looked
> through the window of Dr Fine's house ... On the
> University campus you have repeatedly loitered out-
> side Dr Fine's teaching rooms, looked in through the
> window of one of his teaching rooms and followed
> him from one building to another.

The charge was made under the 'Major Offences' section
of the Disciplinary Regulations. Attached to the notice of
disciplinary proceedings was a 'record of incidents'
based on my reports and a copy of the Disciplinary
Regulations. The hearing was arranged for 17 March
1995.

Mrs M's response to the university was customarily
forthright. 'I have never read such a load of nonsense'
was her summary of the allegations. She put forward a
number of interlocking arguments in defence of her
actions. The first was that the category of 'Major
Offences' under which she was being charged was
'farcical' since the examples given under this heading
only included criminal offences and none of the offences
she was charged with were criminal in nature. Her
second objection was that her actions – 'driving past,
walking past, waiting for someone ... looking toward a

window' – did not amount to harassment. The third was that what she did in her own time and in her private life had nothing to do with the university. And lastly she claimed the right to use the common land opposite my house as well as the different buildings in the university without being answerable to anyone. In short, I might find her behaviour objectionable but she insisted she had the right to pursue it.

Less credibly, Mrs M also appealed to the language of chance and coincidence. It was a 'simple coincidence' if I happened to be in my bungalow at the time that she was enjoying the common or if she were in a university building at the same time as myself. It was chance, looking for an address of a rock group which her daughter liked, that first brought her and her husband outside my house. It was another chance, waiting for her daughter, that brought her outside my teaching room. It was chance, using the local postbox, that led her on another occasion to walk down my road. It was chance, looking for her tutor, that brought her near my office. It was the pursuit of leisure, at the swimming pool and the pub, that brought her regularly past my house. It was chance, rushing for a lift, that made her run past me as I was walking from one building to another.

Whether out of paranoia or malice, she argued, I was seeking to construe an innocent set of coincidences into a pattern of harassment. In effect she reversed the source of the problem: 'Dr Fine just does not like me and resents my presence wherever he is.' And she reversed the order of observation: 'How can Dr Fine know whether I am outside or not? Could it not be a fact that he is looking out for me (all the time) and that is how he knows; he seems to be observing me an awful lot; who is watching who? . . . I was not watching him: he was watching me.' The question of 'who is watching who and why' came up repeatedly in her account. I was trying to turn common land into my private domain. I was even prepared to use an official complaint to stop her enjoyment of it.

Mrs M wrote to the Lord Chancellor's Department describing the charge against her as 'preposterous':

> It would seem I am not allowed to drive past, walk past or stand near Dr Fine's house . . . because this will infringe the proper relationship between a member of the academic staff and a student.

Her focus was on the abuse of power and privilege by the university. She said the university was 'extending their privileges beyond their justified jurisdiction' and that she was sure that the 'timely coincidence' between this charge and her appeal on her failed examination mark was designed specifically to discredit her.

The hearing was held in the main administrative building of the university, known as Senate House. The room was familiar to me but must have appeared quite formal and imposing to one not used to it. Mrs M was accompanied by her lawyer, Simon Wengraf, and with special permission her husband, Angus. Two significant points were put by her lawyer at the start. First, he sought permission for Mrs M to tape the proceedings. After some argument this request was denied and instead a written record was taken by the secretary to the committee. Second, he challenged references in the background documentation to the criminal acts of vandalism and theft of which Mrs M was not formally accused. Speaking for the university, Jim Rushton argued that these incidents were mentioned only as background to the case, and the challenge was rejected.

Jim charged Mrs M with 'systematic harassment' and with 'disorderly behaviour which seriously affected good order within or without the university' – a wording designed to conform to the pertinent sub-paragraph of the regulations. To define 'harassment', he appealed to *Chambers Dictionary*: to distress, to annoy, to pester. This was not in itself very helpful but the main emphasis was on the *accumulation* of incidents, each of which by itself might not amount to much. It was a long day as the witnesses, including myself, waited in another room to be called. I was called first.

It was uncomfortable to give evidence in front of my stalker(s), but also satisfying to confront her and cover the ground. In his cross-examination Wengraf plugged hard on the theme that the road and common outside my house as well as the university campus were all public land and that Mrs M had every right to be there, whether I liked it or not. My reply was that every right, including the enjoyment of public land, has its limits and she did not have the right to stalk me. Wengraf then challenged the use of the word *stalking* to describe Mrs M's behaviour, on the grounds that every one of the incidents might have been coincidental and each incident taken on its own could be given an innocent interpretation. I said that the accumulation of incidents made it highly improbable that they were chance encounters or innocent acts: it is one thing to walk by my house but another to walk up and down repeatedly looking into my window. In any case I argued that Mrs M and her husband had made their view quite clear in front of witnesses that I had brought this problem on myself through my 'professional misconduct'.

Asked by the committee how I *felt* about what was happening, I said that I had a mixture of responses: sometimes I found her persistent presence anxiety-forming and threatening, sometimes eerie and creepy, sometimes I was enraged by her intrusiveness, sometimes merely irritated by the time that I had to waste on it, sometimes bemused by what drove her, sometimes fatalistic that it would go on for ever, sometimes depressed about what this squalid business said about my own life. Overall, I said I dealt with being stalked by putting it as far out of mind as possible.

At this point Mrs M interrupted to say that what worried me was only the 'threat of exposure' and that I had been round to their house many times (in fact I had been once). She added: 'Dr Fine is looking out for me. If he does not want to be watched, he should close his curtains.' It is true that my bungalow windows are open to the world and I was reluctant to put up net curtains which have never been to my taste. Later I put net curtains in my dining room so that I could at least blot her out while having breakfast, but I realised then that I found her gaze less disturbing than the sheer persistence of her presence.

My neighbour, Sandra Martin, testified to the considerable periods of time that Mrs M had been outside my house. Strangely, Wengraf questioned her relation to the university on the grounds that she had used the familiar phrase 'Dear Cathy' in her letters, and challenged the authenticity of her signatures on the ground that her two signatures looked different from one another. Mrs Martin tried to put him right on both counts. Equally strangely,

Mrs M intervened to ask her why she reported incidents to me which she knew would add to my worries and how she could know who was outside her house in the dark. She still seemed to resent the intervention of others in what was to her a private affair. Mrs Martin said that she had told me nothing between July 1994 and January 1995 and that she had first made her observations in the lighter evenings.

Bill Elkin, the university security officer, gave evidence that my steering wheel had been sheared off and that he had seen Mrs M carefully examining my car. Wengraf challenged his identification of Mrs M and later in the proceedings Mrs M again challenged whether he could have had a photograph of her in his possession since, she claimed, there was none on file. An on-the-spot investigation was made and it transpired that Mrs M had twice visited the Academic Office where student files are kept, to ask for her photo back. She said to the clerk that she wanted to replace it with a better one and eventually the clerk sent it to her. No replacement had been sent back. It was unclear whether there was a photo on file at the time when Bill Elkin was observing her in the multi-storey car park, but no one on the committee doubted his word. Mrs M also said that she had contacted the police and that none of the incidents concerning my car had been reported to them or recorded on the police computer. Jim Rushton said he thought the university was in a better position to know what it had reported to the police than Mrs M.

By this time Mrs M was getting annoyed. She asked Jim Rushton, 'Who is that woman sitting next to you?' and, 'Why is she sitting in judgment?' When told that this woman was Jim's assistant, Mrs M said that she was not assisting him.

Alan Norrie, who by this time was Professor of Criminal Law in Queen Mary and Westfield College, told of the altercation which he and I had with Mr and Mrs M near my house. He said he wanted to make Mr M see that his wife was stalking me and that he had a responsibility to 'recognise this on his wife's behalf if she were to avoid the problems that would arise from a continuation of her behaviour'. The difficulty was that Angus could not see this. So when Alan reiterated to Mr M that his wife's allegations against me had been properly heard and dismissed, Mr M's only response was 'Bollocks.'

Mrs M testified on her own behalf. She said that she and her husband used the area near my home for their own reasons – to enjoy the common, pub and leisure centre, to use the postbox, to help one of their daughters who was looking for the office of a rock group, etc. – and that in any case she had the right to go there 'because' I did not want her to. She said she first learnt where I lived in June 1994 (the month of the sexual harassment hearing) when she saw me 'by chance' walking my dog. All she had to do, however, was walk past my house for me to react. She couldn't understand why I had such a 'fixation' about her and why I should be so distressed by someone outside my house. She insisted that there was no connection between her presence near my home and office and the sexual harassment case – that was all in my mind.

To every question she had an answer.

Why did she start coming to my area only after the sexual harassment case? Because she had more time on her hands after her mother was put in a home.

Why was she walking outside my house at nine o'clock on a winter's evening? She was returning to her car.

Why did she park down my road? Because it distressed me if she drove past my home.

Why was it better to walk rather than drive past my home? She was going to the leisure centre and had the right to walk where she wanted.

Why did my neighbour corroborate that Mrs M was harassing me? Because I was a friendly person and Mrs Martin was well disposed towards me. In any event she could prove that it was impossible to see the street from the Martins' bungalow as Mrs Martin had suggested in her evidence.

How would Mrs M feel if the situation were reversed? If she lived near a park, she would expect frequent visitors.

Why was she seen nine times near my teaching rooms and office? She invoked lunch, phone calls, post, daughter, mistaken routes, searching for a room, etc.

Why on Thursday mornings had she been regularly outside my seminar room on the third floor of the Humanities building? She had only been there on one occasion and that was by mistake.

Why was she found examining my car in the multi-storey car park? The security guard had incorrectly identified her and in any case she was not accused of harassing my car.

Why did she continue to make her presence felt

near my home when she knew that I saw it as harassment? Because she was the type of person who saw her 'freedom to do as she wished' as more important than my concerns.

When Angus took the stand, the burlesque was resumed.

Why did they go near my home? To watch the wildlife and enjoy the facilities.

Why did they walk past my house? Because they parked a long way from it to avoid me.

Why did I think that they were harassing me? I must have been deliberately looking out for him and his wife.

Why did they come to the common late at night in winter? Because it was quiet then – the nicest part of the day.

Why did he say to Professor Norrie that I had brought this problem on myself? Because he believed the tribunal was a kangaroo court, but that the sexual harassment case had nothing to do with their use of the area near me.

My own impression was that Mrs M believed strongly in her own defence as well as in her capacity to outwit the committee, and that Mr M was mainly trying to please his wife.

Jim Rushton summed up the case for the 'prosecution'. He said that the suggestion that all the reported incidents were merely coincidental was stretching the credulity of the committee to breaking point – the odds were worse than those of winning the National Lottery. The real

motive for her behaviour was dissatisfaction with the
university's handling of her charge of sexual harassment
against me and her conviction that justice was still to be
done. It was clear that I was distressed and annoyed –
any reasonable person would be. I had repeatedly
written letters to the university asking for action to be
taken against Mrs M and I had spoken repeatedly to the
police. Both I and the university had repeatedly warned
Mrs M of the seriousness with which her activities were
viewed. On every occasion she replied that she was
answerable to no one and would continue to do as she
wished. Jim Rushton asked for Mrs M's registration as a
student to be terminated. Mrs M said this was fine, as she
could now do what she liked.

In summing up for Mrs M, Simon Wengraf argued
that, taken separately, the alleged incidents were insignificant and taken together the case that they added up
to harassment was not proven. Even if Mrs M's behaviour were treated as harassment, it was not 'riotous or
disorderly conduct' or any other 'major offence'. Many of
the alleged incidents had taken place away from the
university and were outside its jurisdiction. The real
problem was my own: I was obsessed with the thought
of Mrs M being in close proximity to me. All the cases of
damage to property and theft were irrelevant, since there
was no evidence of Mrs M's involvement. The connection
between these incidents and the case of sexual harassment was only in my mind – as far as Mrs M was
concerned, the case was closed. It was my obsession, not
hers, that the evidence pointed to.

Wengraf seemed to me to present a plausible case. The
decision of the Discipline Committee, however, was
unanimous: it found the charge against Mrs M proven.

The penalty was to suspend Mrs M from the university for a year and review at the end of the year whether she should be permitted to resume her studies or be expelled. In the meantime, she was recommended counselling.

Mrs M was furious with the decision and resigned immediately from the university:

> After the unsubstantiated and groundless accusations made against me and not substantiated by the Disciplinary hearing I RESIGN. This is effective as from the 16th March 1995, therefore your tribunal is and was useless and unnecessary, because I had already decided to do this anyway ... Dr Fine brought incidents into the tribunal which were unrelated to anything concerning the University. He needs counselling.

She said that the university's committees 'consist of biased members giving a pre-decided outcome' and reaffirmed her basic position: that she was a 'free citizen' and that the university did not have any jurisdiction outside campus. She demanded from the university a copy of the 'undoctored' minutes and complained to the Lord Chancellor about this 'pre-decided outcome':

> I am a free citizen and ... nothing I have done has ever broken any law ... I am powerless to do anything about what has happened to me but I will continue to use both the campus for academic sources and entertainment and Leamington for leisure activities.

In other words, she was not going to stop stalking me. When the minutes arrived over a month later (they were a lengthy document), Mrs M questioned both their delay and their validity, claiming that there were 'inaccuracies and deliberate omissions'. She again wrote to the Lord Chancellor formally appealing against the decision. She said she had been charged with 'seriously affecting good order within and without the university' simply for using the public amenities in Leamington Spa and for spending 'one hour at Warwick University on a Thursday morning'. She said that such a charge, even if proven, did not amount to a 'major offence' and that the charges of property damage and theft were unsubstantiated and tantamount to libel. She said she would never have been employed by the police if she had consorted with known criminals and that it was ridiculous to think that she could have broken off the steering column from my car. She said that although she was not charged with such criminal activity, it was used as evidence against her: 'This is intimidation and I protest most strongly.' She said that both the members of the committee and the witnesses brought to it were biased because they were friends or at least 'willing compatriots' of mine who referred to me as 'Robert'. And she said that the university was abusing its privileges: 'Has no one really any power over these people? ... As far as intimidation or harassment goes the University of Warwick are Stars and their Committee hearings are acted out distortions of the Statutes and Regulations they claim to uphold. It certainly proves the extent they will go to protect this man.' Her own solicitor, she added, could verify how the hearing was 'fixed and decided' even before she entered the room.

Despite the force of her indignation, neither I nor the officers of the university believed that Mrs M had any chance of success with her appeal, but we were wrong and failed to recognise the grounds of her protest.

By contrast, the Lord Chancellor, Lord McKay, took the appeal very seriously. First, he asked the university to comment on why it had introduced evidence of criminal acts to support its charge of harassment. Jim Rushton wrote back that he had not claimed that Mrs M was responsible for these criminal offences but only that I had felt that the incidents might be related to the harassment and that he had referred to them only in reply to questions about my 'state of mind'. Second, he asked the university to comment on why the charge had been brought under the category of 'Major Offences'. Jim Rushton argued that the examples of criminal acts given under the regulations were not intended as an exhaustive list. Third, he asked the university to comment on why it thought it had jurisdiction over offences occurring off campus. Jim Rushton replied that the conduct in question 'clearly affected someone in his capacity as a university member' and that it was for this reason that the university claimed the right to intervene. There was no procedural unfairness, he argued; Mrs M simply did not like the outcome.

In a long series of letters to the Lord Chancellor's Department, Mrs M and her solicitor gradually refined their objections to the hearing. Their strongest argument was that the evidence concerning damage, theft and break-ins was not only irrelevant to the charge of harassment but now also recognised by the university as irrelevant. These events, and not Mrs M's alleged activities, they claimed, may have been responsible for my distress and their admission as evidence made a clear judgment on harassment impossible. They also developed their argument that the 'Major Offences' regulation was inappropriate for a charge of harassment and that the university does not have jurisdiction over what takes place on common land off campus. Mrs M wrote of her strong belief that her original complaint of sexual harassment was linked with the reduction of her course marks. She insisted that all three cases – her allegation against me of sexual harassment, her appeal against the failed examination mark and the charge against her of harassment – were closely related. Finally Wengraf called for Mrs M's resignation to be treated as 'constructive' in that it was only brought about by the university's decision to suspend her. If her suspension were withdrawn, so too could her resignation be.

Above these plausible protests, Mrs M began to pile on more intemperate objections. Why mention anxiety about my child's safety? This was 'quite ridiculous'. Why did my neighbour have two different signatures? One at least was false. Why was there no mention in the minutes that it was 'disproved' that she had followed me from building to building? Why were the minutes of the hearing falsified? She demanded a photocopy of the handwritten version. Most outlandlishly, was Professor Norrie who he said he was? This was her wildest card. She demanded more time to 'conclusively prove that there is no Prof. Norrie' and that 'as a fictitious person, by name, the whole credibility of the case crumbles'.

Mrs M again wrote to Buckingham Palace, on 10 April 1995:

I am the Queen's loyal subject and believe I am entitled to use the amenities and facilities in any area providing I pay for them. I defend my Right to do this and refuse to submit to an unjust and pre-decided 'Court' over my choice which in no way is criminal.

The Queen's representative assured her that her papers had been very carefully noted. She then wrote again to her MP, John Butcher, asking him whether he had been told of the 'criminal offences' in which the university had sought to implicate her and which amounted to 'defamation of character'. In typically robust fashion, she described herself as someone 'prepared to fight for my name and the right to use public areas freely' and complained of 'gross miscarriage of justice'.

She wrote to the Data Protection Registrar claiming abuse of confidential data by the university and myself. And she sent a further series of missives to the Lord Chancellor: one complaining that my application for an injunction was designed to stop him from reaching a decision on her appeal; one linking me to an unknown caller, supposedly from a law firm, who notified BT that her husband had died (my object, she said, was 'maximum inconvenience and disruption'); one accusing my neighbour of coming out menacingly towards her on the pretext of taking her dog for a walk; one complaining that I had tried to get swimmers and staff to watch her at the leisure centre and stop her using the pool; one saying that her presence could not be intimidating since 'he is a man of superior strength ... he has a higher status and he is more influential than myself ... It is me who is intimidated and harassed by his actions'; and finally one saying she would continue to use my area with as much frequency as she believed necessary to uphold her legal rights.

The Lord Chancellor's determination in the case came through on 25 September 1995. To my dismay and that of the university, he upheld the crucial part of Mrs M's appeal: that the admission of evidence of criminal offences was 'so unfair as to invalidate the whole of the proceedings'. He also upheld Mrs M's claim that the proceedings should have been tape-recorded, so that there could be a record of the hearing which 'will be accepted as reliable by those who were present and can be relied on as an accurate and undisputed record by those who were not'. He said it was unwise for a university to attempt to deal with issues which involve it in determining whether or not criminal offences or civil wrongs have been committed, since 'these are properly matters for the criminal and civil courts to determine'. And he judged this particular case to be 'essentially a private dispute' even though we were both members of the university.

The long and short of it was that the Lord Chancellor declared the proceedings a 'nullity', ordered that the decision be set aside and left it open for Mrs M to apply for further 'relief'.

The university officers were very put out by this adverse judgment, Mrs M let no opportunity slip for mentioning what she saw as her exoneration, and I was ever more worried that she could now stalk me with impunity. I felt it was a major defeat. What is more, the Lord Chancellor sent the petition, pleadings and judgment to the civil court where by this time I had initiated legal action against Mrs M, so I was also concerned about its impact on my attempt to get an injunction. In retrospect, it seemed to me that the university had mishandled one aspect of the case in particular: either the criminal acts should have been clearly put as allegations or they should not have been admitted as evidence at all. I had mistakenly thought that we had gone for the first option.

Meanwhile, the university took advice from its lawyers about the Lord Chancellor's ruling. I could not disagree with one of the lawyers from Martineau Johnson when she wrote that 'it was open to the Lord Chancellor to come to the conclusion he did on the basis of the papers which were before him' and that 'he was entitled to give the student the benefit of the doubt and take the view that the Committee may well have been swayed by the admission of prejudicial evidence'. The problem, as she saw it, was one of 'transparency': the committee should have disregarded the reports of theft and vandalism but there was no evidence it had done so. Her recommendation that the university make its disciplinary practices more transparent seemed fine to me. I was also pleased to see that the university lawyers now disagreed with the Lord Chancellor's comment that it was 'essentially a private dispute' in which the university should not have intervened.

Mrs M wrote to the Lord Chancellor asking for clarification of what was meant by 'relief'. The gist of the reply, as I understand it, was that the disciplinary charges were not dismissed, only that they should be treated as if they had not been heard, and that it was open to Mrs M to apply for specific relief once she had decided what she wanted to do. In late September 1995 she sought reinstatement as a student for the fast-approaching new academic year but added a new condition – that all her remaining courses should be free of charge or she should get her money back for the fees she had already paid. She described this as compensation for the inconvenience and legal costs she had borne.

At a meeting with the lawyers, where I was present, three options were considered in relation to Mrs M's reinstatement: the first was for the university to refuse to have her back at all (for example, on the ground that she had resigned or that her terms were unacceptable or that there were civil proceedings outstanding between herself and me); secondly, for the university to have her back but, with new and better procedures in place, take further disciplinary action; and thirdly 'to have her back on the basis she suggests in her letter', that is, without payment of fees. This was the option favoured by the lawyer: 'I know this sounds completely supine,' she wrote, 'but every other course of action is . . . inevitably going to be faced with the type of challenges from Mrs M which will lead you back to the Lord Chancellor.' Consider the management time and inconvenience caused by a continuing fight, she advised the university.

I was not happy with this cautious lawyering. My own interest lay in the university taking a more robust stance. I could see no reason why the university should agree to her financial terms for reinstatement since this was not part of the Lord Chancellor's determination, nor why it should not take immediate disciplinary action if she were reinstated. After much haggling a compromise was agreed: in October 1995 the university acknowledged Mrs M's right to reinstatement as a part-time student but told her that she would be liable for normal fees. And so the matter rested for several months.

During this time Mrs M did not stop coming on to campus. Her presence was monitored by the security staff, who did their best to keep her away from me, while she complained of harassment to the head of security and threatened legal action. She also complained to the Students' Union that she was not receiving 'equal treatment' at the hands of the university but then redirected her complaint towards the Students' Union itself for its own 'negative attitude'. In particular, she accused the students who had sat on the Discipline Committee of representing the University of Warwick rather than the Students' Union and demanded that they be 'severely chastised and reminded of a Union's purpose'. Whatever happened to solidarity? was her closing line.

It was during this time that Mrs M employed a private detective to investigate whether Professor Alan Norrie was really George Cuthbertson, who had an address near mine and owned a white Scottie dog. Claiming that I had perjured myself in my sworn statement to court, she wrote to the Home Office on 15 December 1995 asking them to confirm 'if there is no person known as Professor NORRIE (either in protective custody or otherwise) but there is a George Cuthbertson ... it is essential that every good citizen should conduct themselves honourably and tell the truth'. She also asked the Home Office to convey this information to her through a Coventry police constable whom she said she knew! Not very proper procedure. Her own private detective was either a poor judge of identity or good at meeting his client's wishes, for he confirmed on oath that the man claiming to be Alan Norrie was the same man he spied coming in and out of the home of George Cuthbertson.

On the swimming side of life, Mrs M complained to the manager of the leisure centre that some members of staff had shown an 'inappropriate attitude' and demanded that all staff stay out of the dispute, citing the advice of the Lord Chancellor that it was a 'private affair'. She asked them to 'try to understand the enormous strain I am under; the need to relax, but at the same time I need to assert my Rights or I have lost my case completely'. The amenities officer confirmed that the local authority had no interest in her private life and asked her in turn not to involve the staff in her personal affairs.

Time passed by. On 18 January 1996 Mrs M wrote to the university's lawyers giving them until 5 February to clarify the University of Warwick's legal position: 'I am not prepared to be further harassed or intimidated by Warwick University out of my legal entitlement of ... costs, inconvenience and loss of earnings'. The university did not reply. It was not until mid-September 1996 that Mrs M and her solicitor wrote to the university notifying it of her intention to re-register 'notwithstanding the fact that she still sought compensation'. Queried by the registrar over precisely what this meant, she replied with customary verve:

Do you refuse to comply with the ORDERS made by the Lord Chancellor? ... Do you refuse to reinstate my Part-Time Degree status? ... Do you refuse to confirm that the Disciplinary Committee of 17 March 1995 was a nullity? ... If the answer is 'NO', then I should receive a Registration form in the post ... If the answer is 'YES' then I will refer the matter to the Lord Chancellor forthwith.

Again the registrar requested clarification on whether Mrs M was still demanding the waiving of fees. Her reply continued the attack: 'There are no terms or conditions that must be agreed by yourself in order for my re-registration. I simply apply to the University of Warwick under the Lord Chancellor's Determination and my legal rights.' Finally, on 10 October 1996, she withdrew her conditions.

There was now nothing to stop her being re-registered as a student. A hastily appointed meeting was held at the university – between its officers, their lawyers, the head of Part-time Degrees, the chairs of Sociology and Applied Social Studies, and myself – to decide what to do. Were we to have her back, and if so, how? The registrar and the university lawyers felt that Mrs M should be readmitted and that no further disciplinary action should be taken in the immediate future. The general idea was that I should serve as a kind of 'stalking-horse' (an unfortunate metaphor) while new evidence was gathered about Mrs M's activities. The registrar realised that this was not exactly a good option for me and suggested (I think ironically) that I should take a year's leave of absence in the Bahamas. I said the suggestion was enticing but preferred to stay in my place of work. Supported by Margaret Archer and Mick Carpenter, the chairs of Sociology and Applied Social Studies, I argued that there was nothing to stop us taking immediate disciplinary action once she returned. The lawyers said this was not in the spirit of the Lord Chancellor's ruling and it was ruled out.

There was a significant conflict of interest between the 'university' and myself. I was dismayed by the prospect of Mrs M returning as a student and the university doing nothing. It seemed to me that it was ducking its responsibilities. The good news, however, was that a strong resolution, put by Professor Jim Beckford, was passed unanimously by the Department of Sociology. It read as follows:

> Fearing that the health and safety of members of this Department would be seriously jeopardised if Mrs M were to be permitted to register for any Sociology course, we refuse to teach her. Moreover we call on the University to take further and immediate disciplinary action against her for systematic and well documented harassment of a member of this Department.

At the same time Jim Rushton wrote to the Lord Chancellor's Department pointing out that Mrs M was continuing to stalk me despite a legal undertaking to the contrary and that my application for a final injunction was soon coming to court. He expressed his concern that my case could be weakened if the university readmitted Mrs M and said that sympathy for my situation among my academic colleagues was so strong that 'many would be reluctant to teach Mrs M were she to be readmitted to the University'. His efforts were in vain: on 24 October the Lord Chancellor determined that the university was bound to readmit Mrs M, though he reiterated that this did not prejudice the university's right to take further action.

On 29 October Mrs M was finally readmitted and registered for two courses: Second Chance Education and Collective Behaviour and Social Movements. The latter was taught by Professor Jim Beckford, who promptly contacted the Association of University Teachers for advice. The AUT representative was not happy with the university's handling of this case and promised AUT support if Professor Beckford refused to teach Mrs M. Jim immediately arranged a meeting with the registrar where he pointed out that he could not teach her for two reasons: first, since she had already taken his course two years earlier and had only missed the examination, she could not take the course again except with special permission, though she could sit the examination 'out of residence'; second, the university had a 'duty of care' to him as an employee and that he declined to teach Mrs M on health and safety grounds. Jim made the dispute a trade union matter in a way that I never had but arguably should have done. The registrar had no choice but to dictate a new letter to Mrs M communicating that she could after all not take Jim's course. Mrs M replied that she would take it by examination only and declared her interest in taking yet another course in the Sociology Department: Sexuality and Society. After further discussions Mrs M was informed that this course was over-subscribed and that in any case it was too late to enter. It was now some five weeks into term and a further hearing at the High Court was imminent. Everyone was waiting for the result.

Looking back over this whole meandering tale and institutional labyrinth, I do not regret fighting for the university's involvement. It had a 'duty of care' to myself as an employee, its support was often energetic, and I greatly appreciated talking with individual officers. On the other hand, this institutional mediation took me into a world fraught with its own difficulties, official interests and legalities. In this setting it takes some endurance on the part of the 'victim' to keep his or her bearings and get a result. Was there truth in Mrs M's claim that the decision of the university against her was 'prejudged'?

Clearly there were problems in the university's handling of the disciplinary hearing but through Mrs M's own efforts and the Lord Chancellor's judgment these had been resolved in her favour. In the end she had formally (and perhaps deservedly) won her case, but the combination of her excesses and the actions of colleagues outraged by her behaviour left her with a Pyrrhic victory.

4
The Trial

It was a long time back, in April 1995, that with the support of the university I first consulted a lawyer with a view to taking out an injunction against Mrs M. The lawyer came from an aptly named local law firm, Wright Hassall & Co., and his name was Andrew Woolley. He was funny, clear and a ready protagonist of 'active lawyering'. He explained to me the murky state of the law with respect to stalking. The gist of what he had to say was that there was no criminal or civil offence of stalking, but that this did not necessarily stop judges in the civil courts from inventing one or attaching the offending behaviour to some existing tort if they felt that the situation justified it. Some cases were successful, others were not. Nothing was fixed and much depended not only on one's ability to prove the facts of the case but also on whether the judge was ready to take an open, interpretative stance towards the law. It was a matter of strategy as well as luck, but the tide of decisions was in our favour. Andrew's attitude was to give it our best shot with a reasonable chance of success. I liked his approach.

Andrew's first act, on 26 April 1995, was to fire a warning shot across Mrs M's bows:

We understand that ... you have purposefully 'stal-ked' him at his place of work and near his home. You are well aware that this causes him distress. Nevertheless, you continue with these actions ... You must clearly understand that, if there is the slightest repetition of any of this form of behaviour, then immediate Court proceedings will be taken against you to restrain the matters complained of and an application for damages together with legal costs will be made.

The warning was ignored. On 23 May I wrote a draft affidavit outlining the history of the case from its beginning and the nature of my complaint. I wrote it up as straightforwardly as I could – without legal formality. Andrew then turned this draft into a more formal legal document and sent it back to me for further comment. He attached my narrative to the claim that Mrs M had been guilty of 'nuisance', 'interference' and 'trespass' affecting the enjoyment of my house and office and sought an order restraining her (and her 'servants' and 'agents', by which I understood above all her husband) from molesting or harassing me, approaching within 30 feet of my home and interfering with my property.

Andrew's translation of my secular account into legal form left me troubled on a number of issues: his assertion that Mrs M had been involved in theft and vandalism seemed too strong (they were only suspicions on my part, not facts); his description of her stalking behaviour seemed too thin; his claim about the effect of stalking on my mental health seemed to deflect attention from the stalking itself; and the 30-feet clause seemed wholly inadequate as a restraint. It was not, however, hard to resolve these differences. Some of them had to do with the unfamiliar language of lawyering; some with not irritating the judge with an excess of detail which was available elsewhere; and some with my lawyer's judgement of how much we could expect to get out of a judge. The reference to my damaged mental health (important to any claim for damages) was excised in favour of a formulation in terms of distress. An underlying trust between Andrew and myself made agreement easy, but I can imagine how one-sided and difficult relations between lawyer and client can be when that trust is missing.

Andrew suggested that we take the case, if possible, to the Royal Courts of Justice on the Strand, and not to a local crown or county court. His reason concerned the complexity and controversy surrounding the law on stalking cases, but this course of action had the second-ary benefit of making it more inconvenient and expensive for Mrs M to pursue her vendetta. In mid-July 1995 I went down to the Royal Courts for the first hearing. In the Bear Garden (the waiting room for the courts) I met my barrister, Ashley Underwood, who struck me as a very good choice. Mrs M, her husband and one of her daughters were also sitting in the Bear Garden. Mrs M made a point of circling me in the courthouse while her husband and daughter glared ferociously. I was glad that I had asked a friend to accompany me.

The upshot of our wait was that her counsel and mine went into a huddle together and after various back-and-forth consultations Mrs M agreed to give an undertaking to the court and I agreed to accept it in lieu of an injunction. The terms were close to what we wanted: not to molest or harass me at home or work, not to interfere with my property and not to park her car or use the footway outside my house. This last clause was no worse than the 30-feet condition. We were spared a trial and I went off to lunch with my friend and brother, pleased with the outcome. All this was legally fine. The only problem was that it made no difference to Mrs M's behaviour on the ground. She was not to be deterred by a mere undertaking to the High Court.

On 25 July 1995 my lawyer sent Mrs M a letter warning her of the consequences of further breaches of her undertaking but we decided not to go ahead with a committal proceeding without further evidence. Mrs M's lawyer denied the breach and responded with a counter-charge that I was harassing Mrs M by calling her and her husband 'stalkers' and 'thieves', and that I had assaulted Mrs M. He said that 'on several occasions Dr Fine deliberately surged past her and elbowed her in the chest area ... such matters will not be tolerated'. The claim of assault was not true, though God knows I had been tempted, but my lawyer (or rather his assistant, for he was on holiday) advised me anyway not to do anything that could be interpreted as provocation. I thought the law was not only failing to stop the stalking but also regimenting my reactions.

On 8 September 1995 Mrs M offered to the court her official 'Defence and Counterclaim' in which she denied my allegations and claimed in return that I had 'assaulted' and 'verbally abused' her at the leisure centre, 'beset' her at her house, and harassed and pursued her as she lawfully walked along my road and the common outside my house. She then sought an order restraining me from 'molesting or harassing' her at the leisure centre or on the common and granting her damages. In the face of these counter-claims my lawyer again stressed the importance of avoiding any behaviour 'that could be regarded as that which she alleges – understandable though your behaviour might be in the circumstances'. It is in the nature of law that every claim (even the best grounded) can be met by a counter-claim and that it forces the claimant to hear the other's point of view. This is certainly inconvenient and requires another effort of will, but I do not think it should be viewed as a weakness. It constrains action but in its own mediated way it also represents a form of dialogue.

Mrs M's next move was to seek a summons transferring the case from the High Court in London to a local county court – mainly for reasons of cost and inconvenience. What followed was a peppery exchange of correspondence between lawyers with hers accusing mine of unprofessional conduct over some technicality and mine responding in kind: 'imagine our temptation to make allegations of unprofessionalism against you – we will however resist that temptation'. Andrew told me that 'receiving a letter such as I did and being able to reply in the way that I did, makes my life almost bearable'. On 17 November 1995 Mrs M's appeal for a transfer from the High Court to the county court was denied and a date was arranged in December for a further appeal by Mrs M against this decision. By this time Mrs M had sacked her counsel (because of his advice that she should offer the undertaking) and was herself writing intemperate letters about the location of the hearings:

> I do not know what you are attempting by this course of action, but the transfer of Court is to be Appealed in the High Court; whereafter the case will be heard in a Court of Law locally. At which time your client the Plaintiff will have to pay that fee, because he has NO CASE.

It was not until April 1996 that Mrs M's application that

she should be discharged from her undertaking was heard at the Royal Courts. She argued that it was meant to last only for a short period and that I had taken no steps to expedite a final hearing. The reason, as she saw it, was that I was using the undertaking to secure my own ends – to prevent her from having access to the common, to get her thrown out of the leisure centre and as a cover behind which to assault her:

I have never threatened, abused or insulted Dr Fine. I have never telephoned him or written to him. I fail to see how I have harassed or molested him in any way . . . it is not in the interests of Justice or reasonable that my Civil Liberties should be impaired in this way.

In a short hearing the case went against Mrs M. The judge said that he could not lift her undertaking since she had made it to a higher court, and that what was needed was a final hearing to get this business settled once and for all. He added that the thorny issues of law which this case raised meant that it should rest in London. When he also awarded costs to us, this was the last straw for Mrs M. As he was making his decision, she prodded her lawyer's agent hard in the back. And as I left the courtroom, an almighty row was brewing between them.

My solicitor sought to persuade me to have psychotherapy or see a clinical psychologist. As late as May 1996 he was still asking me with some impatience whether I had yet done so and emphasised that if we were to include a claim for damages, we had to move quickly. Kindly, he added, 'Of course I am sure you will appreciate I understand fully the reasons for the delay.' His concern was legal rather than therapeutic: to secure evidence of the 'damage' which being stalked had done. For a long time I failed to take his advice. The reason, I think, was that under stress I tend to fall back on normal routines and was pretending that the ordeal had not psychologically affected me. But I also resisted transferring the question of mental illness from the stalker on to myself and resented the way in which the legal question of damages was pushing me into a corner into which I did not wish to go.

In the summer of 1996, however, I finally went for some sessions with a psychotherapist. I certainly found it useful, almost enjoyable, to tell him of the stalking – how I felt, how it fitted into my 'real' life and relationships, how it served as a metaphor for a wider and deeper set of issues concerning my past. I began to recognise the dangers of 'co-dependence' – that I might become (or was becoming) psychologically tied to the obsessions of the stalker and dependent on this destructive relationship. I was not convinced, however, when my therapist assured me that this persecutive woman would disappear from my life as soon as I got to the bottom of what was making *me* hold on to *her*. I told him that it would take something more than my own emotional growth (however much this was needed in its own right) to rid myself of this unwanted visitor to my life, and I felt a little aggrieved by what struck me as an excessive subjectivism. None of this could be resolved since my therapist had to go to America for an extended visit and I went off to arrange the final injunction with my lawyer. Despite our differences I missed seeing him and still had nothing to show my solicitor to prove 'damage'.

I drew up my long list of witnesses, revised the

affidavit and made an offer of settlement: I would abandon my claim for damages and not pursue my claim for costs if Mrs M consented to the terms of the injunction. This offer was spurned and the hearing scheduled for 1 November 1996 – some one and a half years after I had first gone to court and three years since the beginning of the ordeal. Time and patience are the prime requirements of any legal endeavour.

Mrs M, her husband and her three daughters (then aged 17, 20 and 22) all wrote statements in her defence. Mrs M wrote of her own troubles: she had spent three years nursing her mother twenty-four hours a day before placing her in a nursing home, and one of her daughters had had a chronic and troublesome illness which required a lot of care. More to the point, she placed the blame for events and for her own suffering firmly on my shoulders. She repeated her primary accusation that I had propositioned her:

> He did not listen to me. I gave him many opportunities to apologise but at every one he refused. Because of this I made a formal complaint to the University. I thought he had probably been getting away with this sort of thing for years and it should end; his colleagues cleared him.

She added a first sign of doubt when she wrote, 'If I misjudged him, I apologise', but she maintained that I had then made 'wild unsubstantiated allegations' about her, enlisted the help of neighbours, colleagues, friends and the public in my campaign of harassment, encouraged people to watch and report her movements and made efforts to monopolise the entire area around my home.

> At every opportunity Dr Fine comes out of his bunga-low, supposedly to take his dog for a walk, then he takes photographs of me or shouts abuse. His behaviour is irrational . . . as a free citizen I go where I please . . . indeed he admits he is looking for me . . . It is apparent that Dr Fine is using his position and the Writ to force me away . . .

She represented me as the perpetual aggressor. Scattered through the statement were comments like the following:

'Dr Fine tried to provoke trouble by bringing a girl, later known to be Jessica Tipping, onto the common land where we walked';

'Dr Fine and Mrs Martin deliberately tried to provoke trouble by coming over to my husband and I and starting an argument';

'Both Dr Fine and Professor Norrie (George Cuthbertson) came toward me in a threatening way . . . I felt very intimidated by their actions';

'Dr Fine brought a woman to my house in a BMW . . . He seemed to be either harassing me or provoking trouble';

'Mrs Volk together with Dr Fine tried to provoke an incident . . . but met with a negative response';

'Dr Fine's office is on the 2nd floor. He must be looking out for me to even notice me . . . Indeed he seems to employ everyone to look for me';

'The disruption to my life that has been caused by Dr Fine's actions and Writ is tremendous, expensive and

time-consuming . . . Dr Fine has refused any action
that would ease the burden on my life such as a
nearer court';
'He has tried to destroy my Degree and make it
impossible for me to return to the University';
'Dr Fine . . . continues to hound me out of the area. He
comes out of his bungalow without the slightest
provocation.'

Some of this was true. I was looking out for her, as were
my friends; I was trying to stop her coming back to the
university; I did go out of my own home 'without
provocation', but why shouldn't I? I did not doubt her
conviction but why could she, who insisted so firmly on
her own rights, not see the right behind my actions? Why
did she present herself always as the victim and someone
else as the perpetrator even under the least plausible
circumstances? Her husband, Angus, was drawn into the
same world view. According to his account, I was 'hell
bent on destroying his wife's reputation' and 'deliberately
provoked trouble'. His tone was one of childlike innocence: he and his wife only came outside my home
because 'the whole area is very pleasant . . . we have seen
foxes, woodpeckers, pheasants and other wildlife'. The
three daughters all followed the same line: Mrs M was a
good woman who looked after her sick daughter and
mother and worked hard, but she was terribly upset by
my harassment of her near my house, by my provocative
visit to her house and by the bruising she received from
my 'assault'.

This reversal doubtless had an instrumental function
for the trial but I also think Mrs M believed it. Every
independent response on my part was read as a sign of

unwarranted aggression. This appears clear to me now. At the time, however, I found it hard to take her and her family's audacity.

The day before the trial started – or was it the morning of the hearing itself? I can no longer remember – Mrs M was standing outside my house waiting for me to leave. As I drove off, she shouted that she was going to 'make mincemeat' of me in court. I arrived alone at the entrance to the Royal Courts on the Strand. Outside was a bevy of photographers and cameramen apparently waiting for some big case; I was surprised to discover that the big case was my own and I was the one they wanted to photograph. It was a new experience to walk solemnly on as the pressmen back-pedalled and asked for more. Once inside the courthouse, I met my solicitor, Andrew Woolley, and my barrister, Ashley Underwood. Mrs M, her husband and daughters were on the other side of the ante-chamber. As soon as I was left alone, Mrs M made a point of walking up and down a couple of feet in front of me.

The judge, Anthony Thompson, turned out to be assiduous and intelligent. He had certainly done his homework reading through the voluminous documents to the case. The case began with legal arguments about the admissibility of witness statements, and the judge made sensible rather than narrowly technical decisions which generally favoured us. Then the two barristers summarised their respective clients' cases. Ashley Underwood spelt out the terms of the injunction I was seeking and Mrs M's barrister, Peter Goatley, outlined Mrs M's defence. His story was that many of the details of time and place within my reports were untrue; I held a grudge against Mrs M because of her sexual harassment allegation; I had constructed a pattern of harassment out of otherwise innocent, coincidental or unconnected events; I had conveyed my prejudices to my friends who were naturally inclined to believe them; and in my developing obsession I then assaulted, harassed and beset her. There was a lot at stake.

I was the first witness and was cross-examined for several hours. Mr Goatley tried to catch me out on details and especially on discrepancies between my contemporaneous reports and my summary of them for the trial. This seemed to irritate the judge, who said that he had to make up his mind whom to believe in this case, not who was the better draftsman. Mr Goatley sought to disaggregate my case by focusing on alternative explanations of particular incidents rather than on the cumulative picture. He suggested that I had formed an association of ideas, for example, linking Mrs M's presence near my car and my concerns as to the car's security that were not in fact linked in the way I supposed. In response I emphasised the accumulation of incidents, including the constant harassment of me, that underlay my suspicions of her involvement in theft and vandalism:

There was not one incident, one frame. One frame would have been nothing; it was the accumulation of frames that made the film.

The thrust of Mr Goatley's questioning was directed at showing that I had borne a grudge against Mrs M after the sexual harassment case and that, wilfully or not, I had constructed the idea of a vendetta out of coincidental and accidental events. I tried to show the court that the nature and number of incidents was incompatible with coincidence. 'She is not using the common,' I said in response to one question; 'she is observing my house, she is lingering outside it for long periods of time. Her behaviour is very odd . . . It does not seem to me to be, by any stretch of the imagination, normal use of the common.' I tried to emphasise that 'each bit of this evidence by itself is not that significant, that what becomes significant is the accumulation of incidents one after the other'. Asked whether all these encounters with Mrs M could have been coincidental, I said that that proposition stretched 'credibility beyond any possibility'. One or two incidents might have been coincidence, but when you have numerous incidents they cease to be. I was also able to add that Mrs M had clearly stated to me that she was doing what she was doing because she was under the impression that I had wronged her, and that therefore our encounters could not be coincidences.

Asked whether it was I who was watching Mrs M, rather than she who was watching me, I admitted that after a while there was an element of truth in this:

After you have been observed for a long period of time, you do get very conscious of it and then you tend to look out to see if she is there . . . But on the whole my overriding desire is to have no visual or any other contact with her.

Asked whether Mrs M had ever threatened me, I said that she had never said anything like 'I will chop off your legs' but that her threat to 'destroy' me was worrying. Asked whether I had assaulted Mrs M at the leisure centre, I said that her claim was simply untrue; what I had done was say to her in front of fellow-swimmers that she was stalking me and should desist. Asked whether I was seeking confrontations with Mrs M, by photographing her or driving to her house or going up to her on the common, I challenged her version of events but basically agreed that I was trying to stop her stalking me. It was essentially this that she treated as harassment. I found the judge generally helpful in his interventions. At one stage, for example, he asked me whether there were many people 'taking a walk' on the common outside my home at 8.30 to 9 on a cold and dark December evening. I said that there were certainly not many and that most of them seemed to have a dog in tow. 'Did Mr and Mrs M have a dog with them?' he asked. No, I replied. He seemed more interested in the general picture than in arguments over whether this or that time was exactly right.

On the advice of my barrister, we cut down our long list of twelve witnesses to five. The first was Alan Norrie. In his sober and settled Scottish accent he told of Mrs M's 'bizarre behaviour' which he had witnessed and of how he sought to plead with her husband, Angus, to 'control his wife'. He gave an impression of academic absent-mindedness when he at first forgot details of his involvement and when in his description of Mrs M's distance from my house he translated what was about 20 yards into 250. More importantly, he confirmed that what Mrs M was doing was stalking me. When asked whether he had sought a confrontation with her, he said that he had tried to 'name her behaviour as stalking and that could have been regarded by someone who did not like being called a stalker as upsetting'. Mr Goatley initiated with Alan a line of questioning which he maintained with some of the other witnesses when he asked him whether he was a long-standing friend of mine and Alan replied in the affirmative. Mr Goatley suggested that Alan's perception of events was related to his understandable feelings of friendship towards me. Alan replied that he had represented the facts as they happened and that his statement had not been coloured by his friendship with me. The judge was manifestly impressed with this professor of law from London University whose actual identity he confirmed, and Mr Goatley wisely refrained from asking him any questions about his other alleged 'identity' as George Cuthbertson.

In his wry, sardonic style my colleague from the Sociology Department, Charles Turner, described Mrs M's behaviour as 'worrying in the extreme' and told of one occasion when he 'questioned her sanity in a rather crude way'. He said it was common knowledge among my colleagues that Mrs M was stalking me. As with Alan, the cross-examination focused on his friendship with me:

Q: It would be fair to say, would it not, Dr Turner, that if you had been given a particular perception of the state of affairs, that you will then fit any actions, however few and however innocent, into that pattern ... That would be right, would it not?

Charles answered that he had drawn his conclusion that Mrs M was stalking me on the basis of the direct evidence he had and that of other people, as well as my word. It was a good question to a 'phenomenological sociologist' whose stock-in-trade is the social construction of reality out of the inchoate flux of experience. The intimation, however, that he fitted the innocuous acts which he witnessed into an interpretative template coloured by my reports, was rejected.

Nicola Wall, my swimming partner, looked composed and smart as she spoke of her encounters with Mrs M and her husband in and out of the pool and related how upset I had once been by the pressures of this ordeal. She was also able to confirm that Mrs M had not used the pool until late 1994. My barrister turned round to me to say what a good witness she was. I nodded and felt terribly proud of my motley crew of friends. When Nicola came down from the witness-box, she told me that there was so much more she could have said. We all felt that. One of the things I learnt about being in the witness-box is that, after you have been asked a question, the floor is yours regardless of the question you have been asked. It is only after the event that the judge may admonish you for not answering. That moment after the question has been put and before the answer is made must be one of potential power for the witness.

Steve Alleyne was a different sort of witness. Black, working class, streetwise, muscular – he looked both petrified and pugilistic in the box. As with my other witnesses, his very lack of rehearsal gave a sense of truthfulness. At first he was rather put out by a string of questions concerning his place of abode. His basic answer was that he used my place during the day in return for helping me out with odd jobs. He had probably seen Mrs M as much as anyone:

Q: Where was she each time you saw her?
A: She might be outside the house. She might be walking up the road from her car. She might be

standing over on the common. She might be in the bushes. It just varies.

Q: Had Dr Fine told you she was in the bushes?

A: I saw this for myself.

I remember Steve saying that he was tired from having got up at five o'clock and having driven down the M1, that the coffee was always good in my house, and that he didn't go swimming in the local pool because he couldn't swim. His honesty shone through.

Bill Elkin, the university security guard who had watched my car, told his story with professional accuracy and confirmed that it was Mrs M who had examined it.

Q: She came and looked at the car and went away again?

A: She had a good old, what I would call excessive look around the vehicle for anybody just passing through . . .

He was able to confirm that the amount of damage my car received was unusual at the university. Jonathan Burns, another security guard, told of how he watched Mr and Mrs M standing in the Social Studies courtyard around six o'clock in the evening for twenty minutes, followed them on foot when they went to the multi-storey car park and walked round all four levels, followed them by car as they circled the ring-road four times and went round yet another car park. They were both good witnesses.

My final witness was Pat Volk. I was very grateful for her coming to court since our relationship had dissolved a year before. She told of the relationship we once had and what she had seen of Mrs M in its course: the stolen car, the drive to their house to look for it, the obscene gesture through my window, the innumerable times Mr and Mrs M walked past my window, their following us on the common and Mrs M calling her a 'tart'. She too was challenged over whether her relationship with me altered her perceptions. She replied that she took my view into account but that she had her own perceptions of the incidents and made up her own mind. She effectively summed up her experience thus: 'I'm not a nervous person usually but I did actually come to feel nervous when I was sitting in Robert's house and would catch sight of things . . .' Mr Goatley also questioned her about my reactions:

Q: You say that when Mrs M was seen, Dr Fine always reacted?
A: Yes.
Q: Would you say he over-reacted?
A: I do not think that is for me to judge. I have not been in a position where I felt that somebody was pursuing me for that length of time. He was distressed by it.

Pat was a brilliant witness to end with on the morning of the second day.

During the break I had lunch with my witnesses, friends and brother while Mr and Mrs M posed for the press, and in the courthouse itself she continued to stalk me in minor ways. After lunch it was Mrs M's turn to do the testifying and Ashley Underwood's to cross-examine her. He proved to be a master of economy. He concentrated first on the very real domestic stresses and strains Mrs M was enduring when she first accused me of sexual harassment: looking after a sick mother, placing her in a home, looking after one sick daughter and coping with two others; doing a part-time job, running the house, all in addition to studying for her courses at Warwick. Then he moved on to her allegations of sexual harassment.

Q: You formed the view, did you not, that he had sexual intentions toward you?
A: I formed that view . . . Dr Fine was cleared. I cannot do anything about that.
Q: . . . Do you still hold that view?
A: No, I think he positively hates me now.
Q: Do you still think that you were right then?
A: Absolutely . . .
Q: Did you take to challenging Dr Fine about his behaviour?
A: I gave him every opportunity to apologise to me . . . If he did not apologise to me, then I thought I should take that further . . . so that it would be stopped.
Q: Did you think you were doing this for the benefit of womankind in general?
A: Yes, if you like . . .
Q: Did you not think that was rather a lot to take on, with all your responsibilities?
A: I do not mind. I am a woman. I am used to it. I do not think it is asking a lot for someone to apologise anyway . . .

At this point Judge Thompson interjected to ask what I had done that she wanted me to apologise for.

A: For his improper conduct and sexual proposition . . .
Q: What was the proposition he made to you?
A: It was a sexual proposition . . .

Q: What did he say?

A: I do not think it is necessary to go into that . . . Has it got any relevance to harassment?

Q: If you do not want to tell me, you do not have to . . . I have read the document and I am still not sure what it is that you were complaining about . . .

A: I do not understand why we are dealing with this document. I thought I was here to answer a question of harassment.

Q: . . . Can you point to the passage in this document which you say was the unprofessional conduct?

A: That was the part when he came over on his chair to me, apart from two other times when he looked like he was going to jump at me . . .

Q: Which page is that?

A: . . . Sorry, I would like to get on to the harassment if anybody is mildly interested in it at all . . .

She said that she was not surprised that the disciplinary hearing at the university had found in my favour, given the imbalance of power and position between us: 'It was my word against his, me as a part-time student, him as a senior lecturer . . . He was cleared by his colleagues.' Asked if she thought there was any connection between her allegations and her low exam marks, she replied in the affirmative.

A: Of course . . . From a 2.1 to a 3.3, yes.

Q: Did that leave you with a feeling of grievance against the university?

A: The marks did. I had worked very hard at those marks. They hurt. Meant to hurt. The other thing was expected. I was not surprised . . .

Q: What were your feelings about Dr Fine at that stage?
A: I hoped I had stopped him doing it again. It does not look like it as he is having affairs with other doctorates. Still, there you go. No accounting for taste, is there?
Q: Why do you tell us that, Mrs M?
A: Just a general observation, that is all.
Q: Intended to wound by any chance? Intended to punish him?
A: Would I? Would I? . . . Such a nice fellow.
Q: I have no further questions . . .
A: Don't we get to the harassment at all?

Mrs M reluctantly withdrew. It was a skilful piece of cross-examination. The motive was established and the hostility towards me revealed. Mrs M seemed angry that she did not have her full day in court.

Angus was very loyal to his wife but did not help her case. Asked about the time he and Mrs M were followed by security men around campus, he said he was playing 'silly buggers' with them and showing how 'stupid' they were. Asked about the sexual harassment hearing, he said the result was a total whitewash. Asked about my case against his wife (and implicitly him), he said it was just silly and he did not go around 'thumping people'. Asked about his view of his wife's hanging around my house, he said they went only for the foxes, woodpeckers and pub. Asked about looking into my house, he said my windows are 'darkly coloured' and the hedges made it difficult to see in. Asked about the confrontation with Pat Volk, he said his wife told her: 'don't come round to our house again, you tart'. Asked finally by the judge about why they did not go to swimming pools nearer their home, he sounded like Goldilocks: one had too many 'yobbos', one was too difficult to park by, one was too far away. Leamington Spa was just right.

The next morning there was a surprise in court when Mrs M asked to be further cross-examined by my barrister so that she could speak about the harassment itself. We complied with her unusual request. After denying stalking me, she was asked whether she walked on the pavement outside my house. In reply she seemed determined to shoot herself in the foot:

A: I make a point of walking on the pavement more now because I have paid a considerable amount of money to try and prove that I have a legal right to use a public footpath, not doing any harm by it . . .
Q: Sorry, can you explain that? You have used which footpath?
A: I use the footpath outside his house . . . I use that footpath because it has been excluded to me.

Judge Thompson asked her to explain. She said that after her undertaking she did not use that footpath for over eight months but that she did now. Mr Underwood asked her whether she knew that this was in breach of her undertaking.

A: It is not in breach of my undertaking.
Q: I am very sorry, Mrs M, I am not understanding a word of this. I thought you said you were using it because you were excluded from using it . . .
A: No, I said I am using it because it has cost me a lot of money, I am the only one who has to pay for the right to use a public footpath which is free to every other member of the public.

She said she regarded herself as discharged from this undertaking, since she had never agreed to it, only signed it because of a barrister whom she later sacked, applied several times for a discharge and had discovered that it wasn't binding because it hadn't been stamped by the court. It was a painful show of self-incrimination.

Q: You have in breach of the undertaking used the footpath deliberately . . . ?
A: I have retracted my word.
Q: Yes, but the court has not let you, has it?
A: But the court has not made an injunction against me . . .
Q: Mrs M, you are always right, aren't you, and everyone else is always wrong?
A: Is that a statement or a question?

My barrister then turned to the identity of the so-called Professor Norrie. Did she still believe that Professor Norrie was not who he claimed to be and why did she hire a private detective to prove it? She said that her suspicions were raised when he 'refused to give his name' at the Disciplinary Hearing (actually his name was on the record), that she had seen him coming out of a house belonging to George Cuthbertson, and that he could not be a professor of law at London University since it took too long to travel from Leamington to London. She said her motive for hiring the detective was to prove that he perjured himself, not to find out where he lived. This was not a convincing line of argument.

Mr Underwood raised the question of abusive language. She denied that she had called Pat Volk a 'tart':

Q: Do you know why your husband should say that you did?

A: No, he did not say that. I was retorting to Dr Fine and it is he I spoke to, and I said, 'Don't bring that tart round to my house again.' But I did not call her it personally to herself . . .

Q: Was she there?

A: Well, in some form, yes.

Q: Was she Mrs Cuthbertson perhaps? What do you mean she was there in some form?

A: I do not like the sarcasm in that. What is your question? If you are going to be sarcastic . . .

Q: . . . Do you carry a presumption that all women are tarts?

A: Of course not. I believe that all women are quite pure to start with.

Q: And they turn into tarts if they are driven round your house, is this it?

A: She came round to provoke trouble with Dr Fine . . .

Q: He has got no right to be anywhere near your house – is this it?

A: He has got no right to bring strangers to my house and sit outside, causing provocation, to say the least . . .

The judge picked up this line of questioning about our being outside her house.

Q: So what was threatening about him being in a vehicle?

A: They were both trying to provoke trouble. You could see them looking, trying to draw me out . . . It was to intimidate me . . .

123

Q: So you think that sitting in a parked vehicle outside somebody's house is provocative or can be?
A: Deliberately, the way they did it, yes . . .

The double standard was almost agonising.

Ashley Underwood then asked her about the truth of her counter-claim: had I really assaulted her? She repeated that I had elbowed her and as a result caused her bruising. He asked her if she had taken any photographs of her injuries or had any independent witness. She said she did not. She was asked by the judge why she did not take photographs of her injuries but she had taken pictures of my house and of me together with children and visitors, and these were part of her deposition to the court. She said that as soon as I caught sight of her near my place I would take photographs of her. The judge asked her what she meant by her own statement of dissatisfaction with the Investigating Committee's reluctance to affect my career, or by the remark which I recalled that she intended to destroy me, or by another that she would never stop her course of action. 'As a free citizen,' she replied, 'I do what I want to do.' At the same time she expressed real rancour about my provoking, intimidating and confronting her. And so it went on. Mrs M had clearly damaged her case by her return to the witness-stand – not least by her avowal that she had knowingly and wilfully violated the terms of the undertaking she had made to the High Court.

Judge Thompson granted me more than I asked for. He increased the restraining order around my home from 30 feet to 200 yards (possibly thanks to the spatial slippage of Alan Norrie) saying that if the effect of this was to stop

Mrs M from using the leisure centre, then so be it. He awarded me damages of £5,000 for the distress she had caused me and costs to cover my legal fees. He said that he had to make up his mind which side was telling the truth and unhesitatingly preferred my evidence:

He was an honest and truthful witness. I am satisfied Mrs M's conduct is an obsession and that it was deliberate, persistent and malicious. She has conducted a vendetta against Dr Fine. It clearly amounts to stalking and ... has caused Dr Fine a considerable amount of stress.

He read out extracts from my diary and said that the proof of Mrs M's conduct did not rest solely on my evidence but on a variety of witnesses from different backgrounds and positions. It was in the nature of the case that most would be friends, since these acts were unlikely to be witnessed or recorded by strangers. He dismissed Mrs M's claims that all the incidents were coincidences or that I had assaulted her, and commented that he found it 'surprising' that Mrs M regarded the brief presence of Pat Volk and myself near her house as harassment given the character of her own behaviour. He said that the reason for her vendetta was a 'frivolous and wholly unfounded complaint' and that after the dismissal of her claim her search for revenge was 'wholly inexcusable'. The time had come for that to stop.

This was the first time, as far as I know, that anyone had won damages for being stalked or had won a restraining order against harassment both at home and at work. It was also the first civil action in which a judge defined stalking – largely in terms of the unlawful accumulation of acts which individually may not be unlawful. He said that damages had to be substantial since it was clear that I had suffered as a consequence of Mrs M's behaviour and because of the persistent nature of Mrs M's actions and of the breach of her undertaking to the High Court. Concerning the other allegations I made, he judged that on the balance of probabilities Mrs M (or an 'agent' on her behalf) was responsible for the bizarre incident concerning the radiators in my home and for the damage to the wing mirrors of my car, but could not be deemed responsible (given that the more serious the allegation, the higher the burden of proof must be) for the other criminal damage to my car, the thefts of my car, the illegal entries into my office or the theft of the computer.

Mrs M was indignant. While the judge was making his judgment, she drew a picture of a person hanging from a gallows with the word 'whitewash' underneath. You could hear her mutter, 'This is the most biased piece of judgment I have ever heard', before storming out. She described the hearing as a 'total farce' and later told reporters:

I have committed no crime whatsoever. I have only driven by his house – walked by. What have I done? Aren't you supposed to commit a crime for harassment? I never went near him anyway. He came out to me.

She was staunchly unrepentant and Angus remained as loyal as ever:

We don't have any enemies, we have never broken the law. We are good people and we are Christians. We believe in live and let live, but Dr Fine obviously doesn't. I love my wife like no other. She has done nothing wrong. She's an excellent wife and mother.

Mrs M presented the case as a battle of us versus them – a 'very lowly working-class person' versus the legal and educational establishment, a combative woman against those who believe that women should be passive and obedient, an aspirant student who wanted a degree against those who abused their position as teachers, a respectable Christian against . . . I am not sure what. She said she had tried to clear her name 'for the children's sake' but had only made it worse for them: 'I'm not a stalker but everyone now thinks I am.' She did stalk me and I am unconvinced that it helps to see this as a 'misplaced' class or feminist struggle. She certainly seemed resentful of those who had more than herself and whom she deemed unworthy of their privileges, and she had now lost her opportunity to get a degree. On 14 November 1996, the day after the hearing, she finally withdrew from Warwick. 'Until the position is made clear,' she wrote, 'it would seem inappropriate for Dr Fine and myself to be on campus at the same time.' And so the matter rests.

After the case I gave a short press conference. I said that I had no desire to see Mrs M sent to gaol but she had to be stopped and it would be better if she received some kind of psychological treatment. I said that being stalked is an enormous invasion of one's privacy – a constant presence in one's life. Sometimes one can laugh and ignore it, sometimes it's very frightening, sometimes merely irritating and time-wasting, sometimes it seems like a metaphor for all that is wrong in one's life. I said I was lucky in having support from friends and the university as well as excellent lawyers. Compared to most victims of stalking I was relatively well off and others would require a 'deep pocket', as my barrister put it, to embark on a similar course of legal action. In strictly legal terms we had made a small contribution to changing the status quo and perhaps made it easier for future victims to bring a successful case. We were fortunate that the judge allowed us to attach stalking to claims for nuisance and criminal damage and that he acknowledged stalking in its own right. It remained an open question in my mind, however, whether it would be preferable for stalking itself to become an offence in law.

The case was over. I did a short interview for television and a few of us, including Andrew Woolley and Ashley Underwood, went to a nearby watering hole to celebrate the result. The wine poured and eventually Andrew and I walked back towards Holborn station. My throat and head, legs and arms were all hurting and I was finding it difficult to walk or talk. I decided to spend the night in London and refused an invitation to appear on TV.

5
Reflections

Stalking is a form of persecution – not the sort of persecution conducted by an authoritarian state like the Roman Empire against Christians, or by a public institution like the Church against heretics and witches, or by a political movement like the Nazis against Jews, or even by sadistic criminals like Rosemary and Fred West against hapless young women – but nonetheless persecution. It is closer to the work of every individual who attaches himself relentlessly to the task of securing the misery of another – through bullying, abuse, insults, denigration, threats or harassment.

The Latin word *persequor*, from which the term 'persecution' is derived, means, amongst other things, to pursue justice to the end and this connotation has entered into modern usage: persecution becomes a duty to be performed in order that justice should be done. In its Roman origin persecution was a judicial action conducted according to rules of law and in its modern forms it retains this sense of its own rightfulness. As in my case, the stalker believes himself to be wronged by those in power and to have justice on his side. In this respect, we may say that he has a good conscience. He declares his victim guilty and his pursuit of justice is relentless. He purports to follow legal procedure, avoid criminal offence and exploit his rights as a free citizen to use public space as he sees fit. His major trait is self-righteousness: he is right and everyone else is wrong.

On the whole, stalking is characterised by the restraint of anger and the coldness with which it is premeditated and applied. It is to fury what slow combustion is to explosion: the violence and anger are still present but as far as possible channelled into effective energy. It develops slowly, progressively, with the stalker endeavouring to secure the humiliation, degradation, flight and breakdown of the victim rather than the direct use of violence. Its technique is to turn the ordinary rituals of public life into instruments of oppression. In most interactions an individual assumes that others will not use their encounters with him as a basis for acts of malevolence. This mantle of trust is part of the carapace of normality with which individuals surround themselves on the assumption that what other people appear to be is roughly the same as what they actually are. The stalker causes alarm in his victim by puncturing this protective mantle and breaking the codes of what the sociologist Erving Goffman called 'civil inattention': those basic interactive proprieties by which we show to one another that we are not a threat and that the other is worthy of respect. When the stalker looks into our windows, he reminds us of the fragility of the day-to-day conventions by which our experience of social reality and of ourselves is ordered and forces us to wonder why we do not see malevolence in any glance from another or any encounter on the street.

In his struggle for recognition the aim of the stalker is not just to watch his victim but to make her acknowledge his presence: the ultimate goal is that she should always be looking over her shoulder. Permanent anxiety is what the stalker demands. He achieves this through elements of surprise, shock, invasiveness and violation: he emerges suddenly out of the dark, he gazes shamelessly through her window, he leaves signs of entry in her home and office, he follows her on journeys, he violates her property and he reveals his knowledge of her most intimate life. Every gesture of anxiety on the victim's part – the trembling hand, the averted gaze, the nervous flight, the uncertain voice – is treated as a sign of guilt to be punished and weakness to be despised. The proliferation of uncertainties – Will he be there in the morning? Is he responsible for criminal acts? How far can he see into the privacy of her home? How far will he escalate his activities – all this compounds the anxiety of the victim. He conveys to her by word and deed that being stalked is a life sentence.

Believing himself betrayed, humiliated, objectified or even destroyed by his victim, the stalker mimics the imagined offence in his punishment. In the act of stalking he convinces himself that he is an autonomous subject, the one who looks rather than the one who is looked at, and attempts to force the victim to act as a witness to his superiority. If this is not obvious, then he has to make it so through his own activities. He has to demonstrate that the sense of superiority which the victim may enjoy is spurious, abnormal, a scandal that must be put right. The triumph of justice in this scenario consists of his public vindication and the victim's apology or humiliation. He affirms the power of the victim as something which only a person of his great strength can overcome – he therefore has to keep establishing his victim as one whose power to do wrong is re-endowed with malevolent energy which can only be contained by constant watchfulness.

With allowance for gender, this is how I experienced being stalked. Faced with the injustices of class and gender, the stalker in my life refused to accept her lot and raged against men and institutions that denied her the material and cultural goods which they claim for themselves. Her anger, however, was lost in patterns of obsessive behaviour that resembled addiction: in the act of stalking she attained the 'high' which set her apart from ordinary life and gave her a feeling of elation, the 'fix' which temporarily eased anxiety but was followed by the feeling that life has nothing worthwhile to offer, the despair that the addiction was beyond control and the unconscious shame that induced waves of panic and self-destruction. Like an addict she took refuge from the risks and anxieties of fast-changing times in illusory forms of moral authority and compulsive violence.

If obsession indicates an inability to recognise the contingency of contemporary relationships, including or perhaps especially the inability to 'accept rejection', stalking is found at the margins of this syndrome. It is not just an individual pathology, but a symptom of definite social relations. Beneath very conservative forms of self-expression, I see something highly contemporary about stalking as a way of life. The relationship the stalker builds is entered into for its own sake and the awareness that the stalker has of constructing herself through her actions would make no sense in a traditional culture where it is normal to do today what one did yesterday. The routines of stalking are not given but self-made. It is the negative index of what the sociologist Anthony Giddens has called the 'pure relationships' of late modern society. As such, it should come as no surprise that stalking, as a distinctive form of persecution, is a recent arrival on the social landscape.

The most likely term to be used by psychologists to explain the behaviour of a stalker like mine is 'erotomania'. In 1942 de Clerambault defined erotomania as a psychotic condition akin to paranoid schizophrenia in which a patient suffers from the delusional belief that an individual for whom he or she professes love, loves her in return. The subject becomes so preoccupied by his feelings towards this object of desire – who may be barely known to him – that this love becomes the very purpose of his existence. This erotic preoccupation has the quality of an obsession in which one individual watches and incessantly pursues another to find signs of her desire. He interprets seemingly insignificant events – the clothes she wears, the glance she casts, the gestures she makes, the time she enters the room, the error she lets slip from her tongue – as proof of her love. This obsession may be experienced by the subject negatively, as an 'erotic horror' in which he feels anxiety, shame, disgust, humiliation, even despair at being unable to keep out the intrusive thought of his beloved. The desire he projects upon her may then itself appear as the sign of a guilty woman, illicit and improper, while his own erotic preoccupation is translated into self-destructiveness. The apparent immutability of this condition led most psychologists to treat erotomania as an 'unanalysable' psychosis.

This psychological profile of the erotomanic subject, again with due allowance for gender, certainly has resonance in my own experience of being stalked, but I am suspicious of a psychology whose definitions of psychosis do not go far beyond the pre-reflective stereotypes of natural consciousness. I find more insight in a humanistic and relational psychotherapy which focuses on the *experience* of erotomanic individuals – and especially on the profound feeling of inner emptiness they report. In the light of this experience it is suggested that 'erotic transference' might be a means of preventing an individual from being plunged into a state of emptiness so desperate as to be akin to self-annihilation. Any break with the object of obsession will involve a confrontation with an experience in which the subject's very sense of existence is felt to be under threat. According to this psychology, erotomania may be triggered by a lost idealised object (for example, a mother-figure who has died) but the catastrophe to be averted is greater than this object-loss: it involves a loss of self in an individual in whom the development of the experience of self is stunted and fragile. The erotomanic subject needs the stimulus of another to the point of addiction and should the subject lose this stimulus, there remains only the feeling that there is nothing inside.

In explaining the 'cause' of erotomania, humanistic psychology looks to factors which obstruct the construction of an inner life – of that 'stream of consciousness' that is composed not only of thoughts but of images, feelings, ideas and memories. We are told that the child's conception of 'innerness' normally arises at the age of about four, following on from that period of 'symbolic play' when the child is absorbed, apparently oblivious to her surroundings. At this stage the child's experience is neither inner nor outer but both. It requires, however, the presence of an adult who can create the atmosphere necessary to the play going on. According to this psychology, the developmental path towards selfhood can be disrupted by a 'toxic' parent who fails to create this atmosphere. Here the focus is on a parent 'impinging' on the child's privacy through sexual seduction, preventing 'separation experiences' through overprotection, withdrawing from expressions of emotion, or oscillating between vindictive rage and depressive withdrawal. Where the responses of the parent are completely discordant with the child's own experience, the embryonic inner life of the child may be stunted.

I do not think that these relational aspects of a child's biography are sufficient to explain how the child *responds* to the situation she finds herself in – for this we need a more psychodynamic theory – but it seems to me to be a great advance on conventional theories of psychosis in that it begins at least to chart the loss of inner life which in adulthood may lead to feelings of nothingness and to the addictive need for stimuli to meet this lack. The main point of the therapeutic endeavour is then to restore to the patient the conditions of inner life. Where the erotic obsession is transferred on to the therapist, this may be accomplished through a gradual process of 'disillusionment' and the gradual introduction of 'reality elements'. The therapist may act as a kind of representative of the external world in her responses to the patient's experience, and not as the passive listener or the narcissistic echo which the patient demands. If this thesis is right, then erotomania may be more 'analysable' than de Clerambault and his followers thought.

Humanistic psychology offers a framework within which to make sense of the experience of the stalker (though I am of course in no position to analyse my particular stalker), but I wonder how far the phenomenon of erotomania can be analysed in psychological terms alone. What are its boundaries? At what point does the feeling of emptiness become a sign of pathology rather than awareness of a world gone wrong? Where does the division between the 'normal' and the 'obsessive' lie? How are the everyday search for meaning and the compulsive search for signs distinguished? How do social distinctions influence the reading of signs? Does not the feeling of nothingness have deeper social foundations and cultural meaning?

In his essay on 'The Elements of Anti-Semitism' the philosopher Theodor W. Adorno drew on Marx and Freud to make connections between the psychology and sociology of persecution. He argued, for example, that the portrait of the Jew which the anti-Semite offered to the world was in fact his own self-portrait: the Jews were branded as absolute evil by those who do absolute evil, were accused of conspiring for world domination by those who conspired to dominate the world, were displayed as longing for power at any price by those who longed for power at any price. For the anti-Semite the persecution of Jews became an obsession; the hatred that drove it could never be satisfied nor disguise its purposelessness; it was an end in itself – even at the cost of the anti-Semite's self-destruction.

It is when individuals are robbed of their autonomy, Adorno argued, that they may hope to regain it through the persecution of others. He put it more evocatively: persecution occurs when 'blinded men robbed of their subjectivity are set loose as subjects'. Persecution expresses the urge for equality in a class-ridden society, distorted into the pleasure of seeing others robbed of all they possess. The self-assertion of the individual is turned into the drive to destroy and immunised against any argument of utility. It may appear simply as an individual pathology which distorts the harmony of the social order but this forgets that it is first the system of order which distorts individuals: it promises happiness for all, but for those to whom this promise remains a lie, persecution can give shape and form to their rage. When they imagine happiness to have been achieved by individuals unworthy of it, this thought can become unbearable and they repeat the suppression of their own longing in an orgy of destruction.

Adorno was referring to a quite different time and place from our own, where violence and Fascism prevailed and no space was left for more humane values. Stalking is of course in no sense an attitude like anti-Semitism, but it is one manifestation of a contemporary 'atomism' in which unhappiness of the self and persecution of another come together in new conservative forms.

The stereotyped opposition between the 'mad woman' and the 'reasonable man' captures little of the interiors of the struggle for recognition between the stalker and myself. I often felt that I was being pursued by an ancient Fury intent on punishing me for the injuries that I had done or imagined, and it is to this ancient imagery that I turned for succour and understanding.

In Greek mythology the Furies were conceived as 'daughters of the night', born of Gaia and the blood of Ouranos' severed testicles, who executed 'ancient laws' and wreaked frightful vengeance on those who violated them. Whether or not the violators of these laws knew of their wrongdoing was beside the point: the stain had to be cleansed. In Aeschylus' *Oresteia* the Furies rose from the underworld to avenge Clytemnestra's murder at the hand of her son, Orestes. They were convinced that a great injustice had been done. On seeing the mother's blood, the Furies fulminated against the matricide:

> you'll give me blood for blood, you must.
> Out of your living marrow I will drain
> my red libation, out of your veins I suck my food,
> my raw, brutal cups . . .
> agony for mother-killing agony.
>
> (Aeschylus, *The Eumenides*)

In their drive for vengeance the Furies were in no doubt that justice and right were on their side:

> we are the just and upright, we maintain.
> Hold out your hands, if they are clean
> no fury of ours will stalk you . . .
> But show us the guilty – one like this
> who hides his reeking hands,
> and up from the outraged dead we rise,
> witness bound to avenge their blood
> we rise in flames against him to the end.

The Furies brooked no interference with their right to vengeance – even the gods had to keep their hands off. Their law was one that fate ordained and was unconditional till the end of time.

Athena's ruling that Orestes be exonerated marked the defeat of the Furies. Her replacement of the ancient law of vengeance by the classical law of the *polis* was presented as the very signal of progress, indicating the arrival of measured and impartial judgment. From the start, however, this new law was born of man and captured by male institutions. As Athena said in her final judgment on behalf of Orestes,

> I will cast my lot for you.
> No mother gave me birth.
> I honour the male, in all things but marriage.
> Yes, with all my heart I am my Father's child.
> I cannot set more store by the woman's death –
> She killed her husband, guardian of their house.

At first the Furies raged against this patriarchal stripping of their powers but Athena's honeyed words eventually had effect. 'You were not defeated,' she says; the verdict was fairly reached:

> You have your power, you are goddesses . . .
> Here in our homeland never cast the stones that
>   whet our bloodlust . . .
> Let our wars rage on abroad, with all their force,
> to satisfy our powerful lust for fame . . .

Athena promised the Furies new honours and they in turn 'feel the hate, the fury slip away'. They soon rejoice in the order of the city: 'joy in return for joy, one common will for love', and everyone seemed content. The 'majesty of persuasion' appeased their fury or at least redirected it towards foreign lands.

In this apparent paean to progress from the primitive to the civilised, however, I think that Aeschylus also put into question how civil was the civilised. In Peter Stein's brilliant production, Athena glitters like some blonde TV game-show bimbo; Apollo is camp, complacent and vastly irritating in his condescension; and the judgment

which acquits Orestes is as arbitrary as it is sexist. The
Furies have, as it is said, been sold a pup. In the new
order of law, we forget why Clytemnestra killed Aga-
memnon in the first place: he had sacrificed their
daughter, Iphigeneia, for the sake of military success, he
had abandoned his wife and other children for ten years,
he had brought back Cassandra as his mistress-spoils, he
had cruelly exceeded his prerogative in destroying Troy
and its people, and he walked over the regal robes which
Clytemnestra temptingly laid at his feet minutes after he
at first refused. There was something impotent, cruel,
wasteful and pointless about him. He had none of
Clytemnestra's strength of character and was easily
twisted round her little finger.

We forget too how Electra, the driving force behind the
children's revenge against the mother for killing their
father, invoked the grief and sense of persecution behind
the relentless pursuit of justice. She was utterly single-
minded:

> Both fists at once
> come down, come down –
> Zeus, crush their skulls! Kill! Kill!
> Now give the land some faith, I beg you,
> from these ancient wrongs bring forth our rights.
> Hear me, earth, and all you lords of death.
> (Aeschylus, *The Libation Bearers*)

She demanded a death for a death but could not do the
deed herself as her mother had done to her father.
Instead she prevailed upon Orestes to put aside his
ambivalence in the face of matricide – the Furies would
dog him if he didn't and dog him if he did – and put an

140

end to his dithering. Behind her demand for decision and action lay a refusal to acknowledge the relativity of Clytemnestra's own crime. All that was left was the category of guilt: 'She killed her husband, the guardian of the house'.

In this new order of things that Athena and Apollo inaugurated, justice was appropriated by institutional authority and divorced from the flesh and blood of real individuals. There can be no nostalgic yearning for the old, heroic order but its memory challenges the perfection of the present and discloses its superficiality and concealed forms of domination. To feel oneself chased by a Fury is an uncomfortable and sometimes dreadful experience; it is as if being stalked is itself a sign of guilt. But it also concentrates the mind on the substance of those ancient laws whose force and ferocity are lost beneath the formalities of the modern legal system.

In the modern world, we are long used to the domestication of the Furies at the hands of Law, so much so that when Fury resurfaces, we readily call it madness and malice. Justice is now represented as blindfolded, signifying impartiality, but the sightless eyes also signify the blindness of a judgment which cannot see the social and sexual inequalities of the actual world. What if the Furies had refused to accept this man-made law that represented the subjugation of women as the height of justice? What happened to their rage? When the new law fails the injured woman, where is she to turn to find justice against wrongs done and imagined? One path is to take justice back into her own hands – with blindfold removed, her gaze fixed on the offending man, ancient laws resurrected and a punishment appropriate to the crime inflicted. Such a woman, convinced of the justice of her cause, scorns the laws of men defending their own vested interests and embraces the ancient law of vengeance as the preserve of women whose rage will not be so easily allayed.

This is a deeply uncomfortable case to write about. How easy it is to sound a triumphal trumpet-call: the 'reasonable man' triumphed over the 'mad woman'! During the ordeal it was my consolation to label the stalker 'mad' but where did it leave me in my understanding?

Being stalked evoked childhood memories and fears, not exactly forgotten but long since allayed. As a child I was afraid of mad women. I recall a dream I had. I was at the bottom of steep and narrow stairs leading to the attic of our house. I was frightened that something dangerous was at the top but climbed up nonetheless. Finally I saw the face of a woman glowering down at me, her veins pulsating with anger. It was my oneiric mother. I screamed and woke up with my actual mother mopping my brow. The headache was bad, the doctor was called, and I was hospitalised with wrongly suspected meningitis. I was eight years old but neither the headaches nor the fear of mad women were easily dispelled.

As a child I recall my horror at seeing on television Mr Rochester's mad wife, Bertha, descending from the attic with her straggly hair, stained smock, wild vengeful eyes, candle in her hands. In this early production of *Jane Eyre* she was the archetype of fiendish unpredictability. It was only much later, thanks to Jean Rhys, that I was able to peer into Bertha Rochester's own possible story. In *The Wide Sargasso Sea* Rhys tells of a white girl, born Antoinette in black West Indian society, who witnessed the burning down of her home by former slaves no longer disciplined by the lash and was then stoned by her only remaining friend – the daughter of her mother's servant. When she grew up and inherited a fortune, she was married for her money, not for love, by the itinerant English gentleman, Mr Rochester. He experienced Antoinette's tropical home as merely hostile and strange. He was a man who prided himself on having learnt to hide what he felt and having repressed his 'mad, conflicting emotions'. He renamed her Bertha, transported her across the Atlantic as a foreigner to English shores, took her money and locked her in the attic as the archetypal 'mad woman'. She had a recurring dream: she was following someone who hated her and made no effort to save herself. Then she dreams of taking the keys, escaping from custodial attentions, descending the attic stairs with candle in hand, mindful of the past and no longer passive. She now sees that 'gold is the idol' which Rochester worships and how much she hates the cold, damp house in which she is imprisoned and the author of her confinement. By repeating the original scene of conflagration which left nothing of her childhood, she recovers a sense of herself as subject and resists Rochester's calls. Now at last, she says, 'I know why I was brought here and what I have to do'. She burns Rochester's house down.

Jean Rhys's view from the attic threw into relief the image of the 'mad woman' I inherited from childhood dreams and fears. In my own theoretical work I explored the proclivity of Western culture to construct a cultural divide between *madness and civilisation*. In a book of that title the philosopher-historian Michel Foucault takes us back to a time before the Reformation when the mast of the 'ship of fools' was the tree of knowledge and the mad were endowed with a special knowledge of what lies beyond the horizon. Here madness was significant rather than psychiatric, wandering rather than excluded and, like the 'morosopher' in Erasmus' *Praise of Folly*, wise in its foolishness.

Foucault asks: 'What does it presage, this wisdom of fools?' His answer:

A forbidden wisdom, it presages both the reign of Satan and the end of the world . . . It is enough to look at Dürer's *Horsemen of the Apocalypse*, sent by God Himself: these are no angels of triumph and reconciliation, these are no heralds of serene justice, but the dishevelled warriors of a mad vengeance.

And for what offence is this mad vengeance taken?

The animal that haunts his nightmares and his nights of privation is his own nature, which will lay bare hell's pitiless truth.

Madness is the mirror which will secretly offer the observer the dream of his own presumption and the pain of his just punishment. When I labelled the stalker mad, could this be the image I had: a dishevelled warrior of mad vengeance that haunts my nightmares and reveals the dream of my own presumption?

Foucault takes us forward into the modern period when the age of reason conspired with new institutions of confinement to place madness unequivocally on the side of unreason, untruth, negativity, uselessness and exclusion. Madness was, as it were, stripped not only of its freedom to roam but of the meanings which it conveyed. It became without further significance – an illness to be locked up or at best cured. Could this be the image of madness I invoked? If Foucault is right that madness tells us something about our own sense of sanity (we who have learnt to suppress our 'mad, conflicting emotions'), then the self-image of the 'reasonable man' will prove more dependent on the 'mad woman' than he knows.

Why me? Was it my fear of madness that drew the stalker to me? I am not convinced by a scapegoat theory based on the proposition that the choice of the victim has nothing to do with the victim himself. Victims are human beings too and 'innocence' is the last refuge of scoundrels.

At one level, I see myself as personifying everything she disliked: the trendy sociologist, the political radical, the unattached academic, the divorcee, the philanderer, perhaps even the Jew. She prided herself on her moral principles, her respectability and being a good Christian; she seemed to see me not so much as someone with a different morality but as immoral and undeserving. At another level, I am told that there must have been attraction as well as hate – some sense in which I represented escape from the confines of her world and possessed an aura which she wanted to be close to.

In my own more paranoid moments I imagined a connection between the onset of stalking and events in my personal life. November 1993, the month that Mrs M began to stalk me, was the first anniversary of my separation from my partner of fifteen years and mother of our child. Like many before, I found the divorce an emotional incubus, as Guilt, Blame, Loss and Anger became my closest companions and dreams of reconciliation clashed with hopes of 'letting go'. It was a time dominated by hurt feelings of separation but also generating a dim awareness of new emotional possibilities. Into this Mrs M imposed her definition of a new 'relationship' – anonymous, contingent, obsessive, violent, full of hate and disrespect – as if dependency on the destructive were the only real alternative to traditional commitments. In my own mind the two dramas came together: the one as inner pain and the other as external manifestation. For a while I felt the vulnerability of one who has lost his place in the world and was convinced it showed in my face, voice and gestures. Did I attract the attention of one who was only too ready to find fault with the 'fallen'? If I had still been living in a long-term relationship, with partner and child, I doubt I would have been stalked. I felt as if the violence of strangers was the only alternative to the fittings and fixtures of a long-term relationship.

At first stalking appeared as a private struggle between the stalker and myself, but I had little choice but to turn to public authority. This movement brought with it an alienation of experience into some sort of 'official' terminology. The articulation of my life felt taken away from me. Language became absurdly formal. Procedures and technical niceties started to assume ludicrous importance. People turned into 'committees' and 'courts'. Once the process began, everything became 'evidence' in a narrative that belongs to a heightened institutional world. Was this appeal to a legal order the inevitable companion to the violence of strangers? If so, it is a bleak and conservative prospect.

At first, being stalked alerted me only to the obsessive violence and need for authority in our 'postmodern' age. I sometimes found myself yearning for long-abandoned routines of Jewish community or alternatively dreaming of escape to mountains far from the cacophonous commotion of our times. I dealt with the experience by not wanting to give the stalker anything, not even my thoughts, but the determination not to let her into my life was achieved only at a cost. Now, in writing this memoir, I have had to accept the fact that I am in some sense letting her into my life in the hope of constructing more flexible and reflective boundaries between my 'rational' Self and my 'mad' Other.

My final hypothesis has little evidence to support it: that I was chosen by this avowedly 'Christian' woman on account of my Jewishness – a Jewishness which found tangible expression not only in my manners and mannerisms but also in the substance of my teaching. I am conscious of having started to look for 'signs' of anti-Semitism: her dislike of my 'whole attitude' was because it was Jewish; her avowal of being a good 'Christian' was opposed to my Jewishness; her complaint that I was wasting time when commenting on my visit to Nazi death camps was because she rejected my anti-anti-Semitic message; her discomfort with the course was because my portrayal of the anti-Semite was too close for comfort. When I received a letter with a Coventry postmark addressed to 'Jew Fine' and containing Holocaust-denial literature inside, I had to fight against the thought that this was linked with the stalker. Mrs M and myself – we were both looking for signs.

Why the Jews? De Tocqueville noted that the French

people hated aristocrats about to lose their power far more than they had ever hated them before. So too in her discussion of modern anti-Semitism Hannah Arendt noted that it was not Jewish wealth, power or privilege which attracted the resentment of anti-Semites but rather their loss. Arendt wrote:

> Persecution of powerless or power-losing groups may not be a very pleasant spectacle, but it does not spring from human meanness alone. What makes men obey or tolerate real power is the rational instinct that power has a certain function and is of some general use. Only wealth without power is felt to be parasitical.

The association of Jewishness, parasitism and persecution made for bad dreams.

6
The Aftermath

The trial received a considerable amount of publicity in the press and on TV. The reports were generally sympathetic and applauded the outcome. On the first day the papers reported my barrister's opening statement and my own evidence. The headlines were predictable.

WHY I LIVE IN FEAR OF MY STUDENT STALKER (*Daily Express*)

'I WILL DESTROY YOU . . . I WILL WIN' (*Daily Star*)

'KEEP HER AWAY' PLEA BY TUTOR (*Coventry Evening Telegraph*)

MALE DON 'STALKED' BY WOMAN (*Birmingham Evening Mail*)

STUDENT STALKER MADE MY LIFE HELL (*Birmingham Post*)

WOMAN STALKER MADE MY LIFE HELL (*Daily Mirror*)

LECTURER TELLS OF 'VENDETTA BY A WOMAN STALKER' (*Evening Standard*)

On the second day, the reports were mainly about Mrs M's evidence and counter-claims:

STALKER ROW WOMAN 'DID IT TO AID OTHERS' (*Birmingham Evening Mail*)

'I DID IT FOR ALL WOMANKIND' SAYS STALKER

(*Birmingham Post*)
STUDENT ACTED 'FOR ALL WOMANKIND' (*The Times*)
DAY I HAD TO FLEE FROM MY LECTURER'S SEX
    ADVANCES (*Daily Mail*)
'STALKER' ACCUSES LECTURER OF AFFAIRS (*Guardian*)
STUDENT CLAIMS LECTURER 'MADE SEXUAL ADVANCES'
    WHILE DISCUSSING ESSAY (*Daily Telegraph*)

I was not pleased to see these allegations about my sexual life paraded in the headlines but I knew they were coming and had no right to be surprised. On the third day the press announced the verdict:

£5000 RAP FOR STALK CASE MUM: 'a "creepy" woman
    stalker was ordered to pay damages . . . the court
    accepted she had a poisonous fatal attraction for the
    50-year-old sociology tutor' (*Daily Star*)
STOP HARRASSING THE MAN, JUDGE TELLS STUDENT AGE 50
    IN REVENGE CAMPAIGN: 'Defiant: stalker vowed to
    fight on after being ordered to pay victim
    compensation' (*Daily Express*)
STALKER WITH 'EERIE GRIN' TOLD TO PAY HER VICTIM
    £5000 (*Guardian*)
STUDENT 'STALKED HER PROF' (*Sun*)
WOMAN STALKER ORDERED TO PAY LECTURER £5000 IN
    DAMAGES: 'A mature student did stalk her former
    university lecturer making his life a misery in a two-
    year vendetta after her sexual harassment claims
    against him were disproved' (*Independent*)
MIDDLE AGED WOMAN STUDENT WHO STALKED A
    MIDLAND UNIVERSITY LECTURER ORDERED TO PAY
    £5000 IN FIRST CASE OF ITS KIND (*Birmingham Post*)
CAN I HAVE MY LIFE BACK – STALKER VICTIM WINS £5000
    BUT WONDERS IF HIS ORDEAL IS OVER (*Daily Mail*)

The *Mail* quoted extracts from what it called my 'diary of despair'. Apart from the normal hyperbole, the only bit of news-reporting that got under my skin was a picture of me in the *Sun* with the caption 'scared' underneath. *The Times* managed to put the wrong photo above what was meant to be Mrs M and many of the papers published an extraordinary photo of me looking like a cross between a ghoul and a political pundit. I turned down a financial offer from the *Mirror* for a copy of my diary but I agreed to do a background interview with a journalist from the *Telegraph* by the name of Cassandra Jardine.

I don't know why I chose this conservative paper which I hardly ever read, but I did. Under the heading WHEN THE STALKER IS A WOMAN Cassandra wrote in intimately dramatic style:

As Dr Robert Fine potters around his house he shoots an occasional look out of the window. A hedge divides him from the street. There is no one behind it. For the past two years, he has rarely felt unobserved. In the morning when he got up, in the evening when he returned home, there they would be: Mrs M, his former student, and her husband Angus, peeping over the hedge. Outside his office she would be waiting to hurl abuse at him: 'Creep, coward, you don't understand anything' ... He tried to ignore her. 'I didn't want them to feel they had won. I refused to become obsessed. I kept reminding myself that I had a real life ... this was something external that had nothing to do with me. But there were times when I wept. I felt it could go on for ever.'

When I read the article, my skin prickled with embarrassment at the pathos which I saw running through both the text and the accompanying photos. I even wrote to Cassandra Jardine complaining that she had somehow demeaned me and distorted my words, but I was wrong. All that happened was that my anxieties about exposure were concentrated in this one rather sensitive and well-written piece. My embarrassment has waned and in any case I feel stronger, less engulfed, less exposed, more at home with myself. Time is healing.

There were also some background articles about Mr and Mrs M. One journalist from the *Observer* went to see them at their home and wrote a piece about how the 'class divide drove Mrs M on quest for justice'. The journalist phoned me up after she saw them to tell me what a nice, loving couple they were and to ask me what I thought about her 'misplaced class struggle' thesis. I said that it had a certain plausibility but that the university takes many working-class students who do well and don't go around stalking people. The misplaced sentimentality of this 'insight' journalism made me glad I'd changed to the *Independent on Sunday*. The *Doncaster Star* drew a different conclusion: in an article on 'women using violence' it cited this case in support of the view that 'women are becoming as powerful as men, but are adopting men's worst attributes – aggression, violence and lack of respect for fellow human beings'. 'That's not feminism, that's stupidity,' they told their readers.

Stalking figured as a theme in the *Guardian*'s review of 1996.

'I was testing her security arrangements,' Bernard
    Quinn commented, after being cleared of a breach

of the peace in January 1996 for having repeatedly
stalked the Princess Royal. The 52-year-old divorced
his wife in the hope that he might marry the
Princess.

'I'm the only person who can help her ... She is
being manipulated and the whole country works
against her ... I want to be her next press
secretary,' said Klaus Wagner, arrested three times
in two months for stalking the Princess of Wales. A
doctor, he was struck off the medical register in
April because of drug offences.

'I'll slit her throat from ear to ear if she doesn't marry
me,' said Robert Dewey Hoskins, jailed for ten
years in the United States after being convicted of
stalking, threatening and assaulting Madonna.

Former Petty Officer Anthony Burstow was jailed for
three years for causing 'grievous bodily harm
through psychiatric damage' to Tracy Sant – the
first conviction of its kind in the UK. Burstow sent
Sant a soiled sanitary towel, stole washing from her
line, poured solvent over her car and sent
threatening letters in a three-year campaign.

'I can't believe this is happening ... he has been
following me around constantly and seemed to take
a lot of joy out of doing it,' said Margaret Bent
after being subjected to cross-examination by the
man she alleged had stalked her – he was
subsequently acquitted.

A London private detective agency, MC Investigations,
started an anti-stalking service based on 'reversing
the psychology of the stalker'; for a not
inconsiderable fee, their gumshoes stalk the stalker.

'Is it fair that a young lady who dressed to attract, the

Queen Bee attracting the drones, the Queen Bee that dresses to kill, cries out foul because somebody finds her attractive?' said lawyer David Stanton unsuccessfully defending Clarence Morris against stalking charges. (*Guardian*, 28 December 1996).

In the *Daily Mail* there was an article beneath the report of my case headlined 'PAMELA' FIEND IS LOCKED UP about a stalker who 'terrorised a Pamela Anderson look-alike'. Described as a convicted rapist and psychopath, he was convicted of causing psychological harm, having bombarded her over a period of eight months with letters, champagne and gifts and twice threatening her with a knife. She suffered nightmares, crying fits and mysterious pains. When the Pamela Anderson 'look-alike' and her father appeared on *Saturday Night Live*, the father threatened to kill the stalker if he ever came near his daughter again. Most people on the show seemed to find this quite acceptable.

In the same year, 1996, the Tory government blocked a Labour member's anti-stalking bill, mooted its own in a consultation document, omitted it from the Queen's Speech, and then reintroduced it later that day. It symbolised the government's indecision in the twilight of their power. The Bill ended its legislative journey only after Labour won the election, emerging in June 1997 as the Protection from Harassment Act.

This Act makes low levels of harassment (like persistent phone calls or sending flowers to an unwilling recipient) a civil offence for which victims could take out an injunction to secure a restraining order and damages. Any breach of the restraining order becomes itself an arrestable criminal offence liable to two years' maximum sentence. It makes 'causing harassment' a criminal offence, with a six-month maximum sentence and £5,000 maximum fine. And it makes harassment 'causing fear of violence' a more serious criminal offence carrying a maximum sentence of five years and an unlimited fine. It allows a restraining order to be attached to the lesser criminal offence of causing harassment and, if any breach occurs, it exposes the perpetrator to a maximum sentence of five years, an unlimited fine and a claim for damages. Legal aid would be made available, subject to the normal constraints for taking civil action.

The Act has strengths: it makes early intervention possible for the thousands of victims of stalking, a few of whom would eventually be killed and many more terrorised and violated. It allows for distinctions to be made between less and more serious cases of stalking and for legal actions to be taken on both the civil and the criminal side, and it makes breaches of restraining orders a serious business with powerful sanctions waiting in the wings. It signifies in its own way that society is no longer prepared to tolerate such forms of oppressive behaviour. Compared to past practices in criminal law when prosecutors had to fall back on the impact of stalking as a form of psychological assault or grievous bodily harm, and in civil law when plaintiffs had to hope that the court would accept the attachment of stalking to existing torts like nuisance or trespass or that it would simply judge on the basis of what is reasonable despite the absence of any statute, the new law promises more protection to victims of stalking and exposes them to less of a legal lottery.

And yet the new legislation is actually silent on

stalking. The word never appears. The original Bill from which this Act derives explicitly made stalking into a criminal offence; it defined the kind of conduct to which stalking refers (e.g. following, loitering near, watching or approaching another person to cause that other person to feel harassed, alarmed, distressed or to fear for his or her safety); it defined the harm which stalking inflicts on individuals; and it wanted the new Act to be called the 'Stalking Act 1996'. Somewhere along the line, however, between the Bill of 1996 and the Act of 1997, stalking was translated into harassment and the word 'stalking' disappeared altogether.

A Home Office Consultation Paper of July 1996, entitled 'Stalking – the Solutions', addressed itself to the difficulties of defining the term:

> There is a risk that if the scope of any new legislation to deal with stalking is not carefully defined, it will criminalise the everyday behaviour of innocent people ... Many of the actions of stalkers are, in themselves, harmless – walking up and down a street, or standing on a street corner for example. There is a need to ensure that new laws against stalking do not, for example, catch investigative journalists, religious activists, debt collectors or even political canvassers. (paragraph 4a)

The then government's recommendation, however, was to legislate in terms of 'molestation' in civil law and 'harassment' in criminal law. A new statutory tort of 'molestation' was proposed which would recognise that everyone has the right 'not to be caused distress as a result of molestation' and whose remedy would depend not on rights of property but on 'rights of physical integrity' – even where the harm suffered falls short of physical injury. Within criminal law, the idea was to extend the offence of 'harassment' under the Public Order Act of 1986 to make it more effective in dealing with stalkers. This meant two things in effect: first, it was proposed that there should no longer have to be any evidence of *threatening, abusive or insulting* conduct on the part of the accused, since the behaviour of stalkers often does not fit within these categories; second, the requirement that the accused *intended* to cause distress or alarm or harassment was to be lifted on the grounds that stalkers often have no intention to cause harm or distress to their victims. The proposal was to define as harassment any conduct which a 'reasonable person' would expect to cause the victim distress, alarm or harassment. Seeing that it is a feature of stalking that the behaviour occurs repeatedly and recognising that such major extensions to the scope of harassment could lead to all manner of activities falling foul of it, the Home Office proposed only to add the concept of 'persistence' into the new legislation.

If the proposed Act posed serious civil liberty issues, the actual Protection from Harassment Act was even more wide-ranging. In it there is no longer any reference to 'intention' or to 'threatening, abusive or insulting words or behaviour': it says only that individuals are prohibited from pursuing a course of conduct which 'amounts to harassment of another, and which he knows or ought to know amounts to harassment'. The words 'ought to know' are defined as meaning that a 'reasonable person' in possession of the same information would think that the conduct amounted to harassment.

As far as I can tell, there is no other attempt to define harassment except to say that it *includes* alarming people or causing them distress. All reference to *persistence* has been dropped except that the conduct must occur on at least two occasions. And no specific exemptions are made, for example for journalists, trade union pickets, religious activists or political demonstrators.

The question of protecting people from stalkers has been translated in law into the much broader category of 'protection from harassment'. This translation is highly significant. On the one hand, it indicates the law's failure to name stalking specifically as an offence and means that stalking itself has once again fallen off the legislative map. How, for example, are the police supposed to take stalking seriously if the word itself is still absent from law? Words are important and in this case the right word is missing. The law conventionally recognises certain kinds of harm like bodily hurt, damage to property, loss of privacy, damage to reputation, etc.; but it has difficulty in recognising the less tangible forms of harm, like those affecting bodily integrity and feeling safe, which an offence like stalking (perhaps in parallel with sexual harassment) raises. Just as the law has typically dissolved sexual harassment into discrimination, so too it is now dissolving stalking into harassment.

On the other hand, the new legislation poses a tangible threat to civil liberties. While stalking another person can never be justified, harassment is sometimes deemed legitimate: as when a journalist harasses a corrupt politician in order to wheedle the truth out of him, or union pickets harass strike-breakers when they go to work, or when peace protesters harass arms profiteers, or religious activists harass their leaders on account of their discrimination against women. Readers will have their own examples of what they consider to be legitimate harassment, not necessarily coinciding with my own; but whatever the list, the question is raised as to whether every individual has a right to be free from harassment. A blanket protection from harassment may sound like protection of people's freedom from oppressive behaviour – and in part it is so – but it also protects privilege and dogma from criticism. This may sound perverse but is not a right to harass an important element in a free society?

Intention is surely crucial in distinguishing between, say, a journalist whose intention is to extract secret information from a politician or businessman and a stalker whose intention is to compel another individual to pay him the attention he craves. Some definition of threatening, abusive or insulting behaviour is surely crucial in addition to subjective criteria of causing alarm and distress. Excessive reliance on the views of the 'reasonable person' detracts from the specificity of laws and grants wide judicial discretion. In American constitutional law, anti-stalking legislation has been challenged on grounds of freedom of movement and freedom of speech as well as the 'overbreadth' and 'vagueness' of its criminal statutes. British lawyers prefer to think about what is reasonable or not and are reluctant to go down the American highway of rights. Whatever the weaknesses of American legal culture, the British seems very uncritical when it comes to civil liberties.

In the last few years stalking has become the target of what sociologists typically call a 'moral panic'. First comes the apparent proliferation of the offence itself, then publicity about its seriousness and frequency (with reports of violence, terror and threats partly based on the voice of the victim), then calls for a tough social response to curb this offence, and finally the passing and implementation of new laws. Sociologists tend to emphasise the mythic aspects of moral panics – the cultural representation of the stalker as a 'folk devil' in the public imagination – even if the underlying problem is real. The myth often reinforces law and order, but it also has wider cultural significance. In the so-called 'slasher film' (like *The Stepfather* of 1987) stalking is closely linked to the male gaze and murder of women victims, but such films are also about the surviving woman's appropriation of violence and the gaze to defend herself and convey the pleasure of retaliation and victory over the pathological killer. In the serial killer film *The Silence of the Lambs* (1991) the woman FBI agent marries intuition and intelligence not to appropriate the violence of the stalker but to comprehend it (in a way absolutely unavailable to the serried ranks of the male FBI agents) and thus overcome it. Now there's a role model.

After the trial I went into hospital for a week for tests. My arms and legs were painful and the muscles weak and I wondered whether there was any connection with the stresses and strains of the stalking. I received lots of letters from old friends and colleagues offering their good wishes and I managed to renew friendships that had lain dormant for decades. This was one of the benefits of the case. I also received a few hate-letters, like one anonymous note saying:

How many times have you got away with it now. You

are the one receiving counselling yet accuse the lady of being mentally ill/cheap. What went wrong with your marriage? May we hear from your own wife. This lady is still with her husband who supports her case. Come on tosser.

As I mentioned earlier, I received a letter addressed to 'Jew Fine' and containing the gems of Holocaust-denial literature. For example:

Did the Jews of the world 'declare war on Germany'? Yes. The world media carried the headlines, 'Judaea declares war on Germany'.

On the other side, I received an anonymous phone call on my answer machine congratulating me on winning the court case and saying that Mrs M 'had it coming to her for a long time'.

Mrs M's stalking activities diminished but didn't stop. In December 1996 one of my neighbours told me that he saw Mrs M near my home a few times 'wearing a wig'; in fact she seems to have dyed her hair darker. Nicola Wall, my swimming friend, told me she had seen Mrs M, her daughter and her husband in the swimming pool. In early January 1997 I saw Mr and Mrs M walking on the common outside my home. She was waving to neighbours and going in and out of the woods. Steve Alleyne and I both saw her a few times driving slowly past my house. Once she waved sarcastically at me as I left the house. One of my colleagues saw Mrs M pacing up and down outside the new Sociology building. In February I saw Mrs M on the pavement outside my home for five minutes until she crossed the road and was picked up by her husband. I think her daughter was in the back of the car, which then stopped outside my house for a minute or so with the horn sounding intermittently. One morning Mrs M was outside my house when I went for my swim and was still there when I returned. She made a point of walking straight up to me – almost nose to nose. I didn't respond. That evening, she slowly drove by my house and made a V sign at me and a guest. The next evening she did the same – drove slowly past my house, turned around further up the street and passed my house again as a friend and I watched her. In March and April Mrs M was rarely seen but in May she started again. Between 14 and 30 May she and her husband drove past my house at least six times. They would slow down in their new black Rover, sometimes wait outside for a couple of minutes, hoot a few times and then park their car near the pub. When I walked Fudge slowly up to the leisure centre, looking from side to side and over my shoulder to see where Mr and Mrs M were and where they had parked, I felt the trace of old anxieties.

Despite the court order awarding me costs and damages, Mrs M made no attempt at payment. Encouraged and sometimes pressed by the university, I instructed my solicitor to go ahead with enforcement – an unpleasant procedure involving the possibility of a sheriff sequestering her goods and of bankruptcy. Andrew's agents had considerable difficulty handing the documents 'personally' to her, as is the requirement of the court. Twice they received no answer when they rang the doorbell although they heard people inside. The third time, Mr M opened the door but shut it on them when he realised who they were. They looked through the letterbox and saw Mrs M sitting in the hallway. The

agents opened the letterbox and projected the papers
through it – a procedure which I am told will be accepted
by the court as proper service – at which time Mrs M
finally leapt up and moved extremely swiftly towards
the agent in an attempt to push the documents back out.
She did not succeed. Nothing has yet been resolved and I
have received neither damages nor costs.

I discussed with my lawyer the possibility of initiating
committal proceedings against Mrs M for her violations
of the restraint order. Jim Rushton, speaking for the
university, was keen that I should go ahead on this front
as speedily as possible, but I was hesitant. I thought there
was some indication, despite her violations, that Mrs M
was trying to control her obsessive behaviour and that it
would be best to go back to court with evidence of more
accumulated violations. I didn't want to be or to appear
to be vindictive, I wasn't convinced how effective a
warning or a few days in gaol would be in stopping her,
and I did not want to be rushed into taking action.
Beyond these reasons I wanted psychologically to put the
case behind me and treat it as an event in the past about
which I am writing from the secure distance of the
present. At the end of May, however, after another bout
of infractions, I did phone my lawyer to initiate committal proceedings and I am preparing an affidavit. I heard
on the grapevine that Mrs M parted company with her
solicitor, Simon Wengraf, and went to many other
lawyers looking for one to appeal the court case. They all
declined. Apart from everything else, I understand she
had left it too late.

I can neither predict nor control the outcome of this
struggle for recognition, waged between the stalker and
the stalked and mediated through law, institution and

now text. But it doesn't weigh upon me as it used to. I think I'm learning to enjoy the present.

Acknowledgements and Sources

I wish to acknowledge the encouragement and advice of Jenny Uglow and Jonathan Burnham at Chatto & Windus, and my friends Lawrence Welch, Peter Wagner, Gwen Norrie, Alan Norrie, Heidrun Friese, Marion Doyen, Alison Diduck and Gillian Bendelow, all of whom have read this text at one or other stage of its production. Their help has been invaluable. I should also like to thank my solicitor, Andrew Woolley, who is now taking on other cases of people who are being stalked (telephone number: 01789 267 377), my barrister, Ashley Underwood, the officers of the University of Warwick who have more than met their 'duty of care' (especially Jim Rushton and Cathy Chaulton), my colleagues and students at the university who have supported me throughout this lengthy and unfinished business, and my other witnesses who put themselves out to attend trials (Steve Alleyne, Jonathan Burn, Bill Elkin, Charles Turner, Pat Volk and Nicola Wall). Thanks also to Tony Fine for his brotherly love.

Quotations are from the following sources: Theodor W. Adorno, 'Elements of Anti-Semitism: The Limits of Enlightenment', *Dialectic of Enlightenment*, London, Verso, 1995; Aeschylus, *The Orestia*, trans. Robert Fagles, Harmondsworth, Penguin, 1984; Hannah Arendt, *The*

Origins of Totalitarianism, London, Andre Deutsch, 1973; Michel Foucault, *Madness and Civilisation*, New York, Mentor, 1967; Franz Kafka, *The Trial*, Harmondsworth, Penguin, 1963; Jean Rhys, *Wild Sargasso Sea*, London, Andre Deutsch, 1966; Ludwig Wittgenstein, *Remarks on the Philosophy of Psychology*, Oxford, Basil Blackwell, 1980. Reference is made to: Robert P. Faulkner & Douglas H. Hsiao, 'And Where You Go I'll Follow: The Constitutionality of Anti-Stalking Laws and Proposed Model Legislation', *Harvard Journal of Legislation*, Vol. 31, No. 1, Winter 1994; Helen Garner, *The First Stone: Some Questions About Sex and Power*, Sydney, Picador, 1995; Anthony Giddens, *The Transformation of Intimacy: Sexuality, Love and Eroticism in Modern Societies*, Cambridge, Polity, 1993; Erving Goffman, *Relations in Public*, London, Allen Lane, 1971; Beth Kotze & Russell Meaves, 'Erotic Transference and a Threatened Sense of Self', *British Journal of Medical Psychology*, Vol. 69, Part 1, March 1996; Jean Ritchie, *Stalkers: How Harmless Devotion Turns to Sinister Obsession*, London, Harper Collins, 1994; Edward Thompson, 'The Rising Cost of Righteousness', *Views*, No. 7, Spring 1963; D. W. Winnicott, *Playing and Reality*, Harmondsworth, Penguin, 1974.

The National Anti-Stalking and Harassment Support Association (NASH) may be contacted at 01926 334833.